PARISH DAMNED

PARISH DAMNED
Lee Thomas

First published in England in 2005 by

Telos Publishing Ltd
61 Elgar Avenue, Tolworth, Surrey, KT5 9JP, England
www.telos.co.uk

Telos Publishing Ltd values feedback. Please e-mail us
with any comments you may have about this book to:
feedback@telos.co.uk

ISBN: 1-84583-040-7 (paperback)
Parish Damned © 2005 Lee Thomas.

ISBN: 1-84583-044-X (hardback)
Parish Damned © 2005 Lee Thomas.
Frontispiece © 2005 Simon Moore.

Printed in India

1 2 3 4 5 6 7 8 9 10 11 12 13 14 15

British Library Cataloguing in Publication Data.
A catalogue record for this book is available from the
British Library.

For
John C Perry

1

I've been here before.

This uncertain, disturbing and downright miserable twist of feelings, when every emotion is another length of rope knotted and tied so you can't tell where one starts and the other ends, is a confusing and painful state to be in.

And unfortunately, it isn't new to me.

There's an old proverb. At least, I think it's a proverb. Maybe it's just something I heard in a bar once and it stuck with me. Anyway, it sounds enough like a cookie fortune to be important and it goes: 'If you travel far enough in any direction, you'll end up right back where you started.' What with the Earth being round, that makes a lot of sense, and since most folks can't navigate worth a damn, a straight course is the easiest path to follow.

And like I said, I've been here before.

When those people came down sick with the crud, I knew it wasn't just an outbreak of the flu like Doctor Davis said, because I'd seen it a time or two. Doc Davis had seen it before too, but I can't honestly say if he knew what I did. We weren't buddies or anything, so we never did chat about the sickness that blew into town every four or five years, or the people, usually the elderly or the young, who started in with the fevers and the dehydration, the shortness of breath and the nasty rashes. A common outbreak usually struck half a dozen folks, and Doc Davis never did find a good treatment.

On the morning that I skippered my trawler out to the reef carrying that fat banker from Chicago, two kids had already succumbed to the crud, and I felt myself getting a good case of the jitters pulling the *Judy Anne* out of her slip at sunrise.

But you make your money where you can, and it wasn't like people had started drifting ashore yet. Besides, that banker, Bentley by name, was a big spender and didn't ask much of a charter. He didn't fish, so I didn't have to worry about wasting line or reels with his inexperienced hands, and he wasn't much interested in learning to captain my rig, which was a good thing because I don't let anyone behind her wheel.

In fact, the only things that Bentley wanted to do was go way out in the gulf, drink a lot of rum, read books and sun his big belly on the deck. That left me plenty of time to do some fishing of my own or just read the paper and drink coffee until he announced, 'I'm baked,' and I captained us back to the docks.

Sometimes, these folks from the north are a good laugh. I mean, Bentley could have sunned and drank and read poolside at his hotel, but he was rich and I got the impression that he wanted to tell folks about his adventurous times in the Keys. He wanted to say things like, 'I went boating,' or, 'I did me some deep sea fishing.'

And he was a good enough guy, I suppose. I'd been taking Bentley out for over six years, every season, but the morning that Morris Planke died of the crud, Bentley wasn't content with his rum-buzz and sunburn. He wanted to chat, and that was fine with me.

'What do you think about this stuff that's killing those kids?' Bentley asked me, rubbing suntan oil over his belly like a Buddha making his own luck. 'You think it's contagious?'

'Nah,' I told him. 'This comes through every few years, and those that got it, got it. You don't have to worry. It's a terrible thing, but it usually doesn't get more than a handful of people.'

'Well, I'll tell ya' something, Cap,' Bentley said. He always called me Cap, like I was an old salt, when in fact he was a good ten years older than I was and had the wrinkles and the white hair to prove it. 'I saw Morris Planke the other morning, and he scared the living shit out of me. I've been doing business with his family for nearly thirty years, and I'd say I knew the old man pretty well. In fact, I only know about Coral Point because he invited me down for a visit after he got that hotel open. What's that been, about twenty years now? Sure, about twenty years, so I know the old boy. Hell, I know the whole family.

'So there I was, checking in to his hotel, and he walks through the lobby like both his hips are broken. You know what I'm saying? He was limping on both legs, sweating like he'd just run a marathon, and half his face was covered in those red bumps. Well, he's an old guy and I figured he was going through a bad patch, but damned if he wasn't a good-looking guy before. Nothing queer in that at all. He was a damned fine looking guy, but when I saw him the other morning, he looked like something had just eaten him up from the inside. I figured he got the cancer or something.

'And when I went up to say hello, he just stared at me

9

like I was pointing a gun in his face and asking for his wallet. His eyes were all wild, and he looked terrified of me. He was even drooling a bit, and it about made me sick, so I excused myself. But like I said, I've known old Morris for a good thirty years, and he didn't seem to have a clue who the hell I was.'

'Damn shame,' I said. My mind was elsewhere, still with Bentley's description of Morris Planke. I knew the kind of shuffling step he had described and was terribly familiar with the vacant, desperate stare coming from faces stained by blotch and bump.

'Damn shame is damn right,' Bentley said. 'I'm not a superstitious sort of man, but I swear I could smell the death on him. I bet he doesn't last the week.'

That would have been a bad bet to take.

As we pulled into the dock, Bentley paid me cash as was his custom, and he said that he was headed back north and didn't think he'd be returning to Coral Point.

'I can't get that smell out of my nose,' he told me. Then, the fat banker thanked me and wished me well before waddling down the dock in the direction of his hotel.

The news about Morris Planke's death was all over town by the time the *Judy Anne* was secured in her slip. A good crowd had gathered at Ethel's Luncheonette and they spoke of the hotel owner's passing in whispered tones as if Death were an eavesdropper who could be summoned should his name be spoken too loudly.

But I was already beginning to fear that the man who had brought Planke's death was long gone.

You see, the crud that infected and wasted folks, the sickness that Doc Davis called 'the flu,' always followed a man named Graham to Coral Point, and more than likely anywhere else he docked his boat. I'd seen Graham's yacht secured at the end of the pier one afternoon about three weeks before that first kid was found all curled and cold in his bedroom closet. I did what I could but, as usual, nobody would listen, because folks just don't know any better.

Tim Planke, the son and sole heir to Morris Planke's worldly goods certainly hadn't wanted to listen to me. Part of our little city's council, Tim Planke was a nasty fella with an attitude as spoiled as any I'd ever seen. He'd laughed off my warning about Graham and called me a few names that a gentleman would have been better to keep to himself, but I imagine he started taking a bit of what I'd told him seriously when his father got in a bad way.

I don't like Tim Planke, not one bit, but I couldn't help but feel a bit sorry for him in light of his father's passing.

'They found Old Morris in the wine cellar of the hotel,' Mizzie Townsend, a stout waitress with a thin nest of frazzled red hair, told a table of interested fishermen. 'They said he was curled up under a rack of his best chianti and looked like he'd just been kissed by the devil. Doc Davis had to all but break his arms off to get him out from under there, what with the rigor and all.'

One of the fishermen shook his head slowly in awful appreciation of the detail Mizzie provided, while another crossed himself.

Funny how some people do that out of reflex – cross themselves – even when they don't know exactly what it is they are hoping to protect themselves against.

After excusing myself from Ethel's Luncheonette, making some excuse to Mizzie, who had hovered over me anticipating a new audience for her gruesome story, I

11

walked back to the docks and checked the sky. A few hours of daylight remained.

Some of the other boats with their charters were pulling in from a full day of fishing or scuba diving. Boots and deck shoes, tennis shoes and sandals slapped the boards of the marina as exhausted families let their legs adjust to land. The water looked blue and fine as a light breeze blew in off the gulf.

My first fear was that I would not see Graham's boat in its slip. Uneasiness followed me over the planks like a shadow. A couple of boys had been found in their homes, and Morris had been found in the wine cellar of his hotel, and that meant something was wrong.

Like I said, this tiny plague hit Coral Point every four or five years when Graham would dock. But those stricken were never found on dry land. Never. If someone showed up with symptoms – the broken walk, the dehydration, the rash – you could make some good money betting that they'd be found drifting ashore within the next week or two, if they were ever found at all.

Some of the older, more superstitious folks had taken to calling the victims 'parish damned,' and thought that something about the sickness drove the dying into the waves.

Purser rigged and parish damned.

The expression is an old one, no doubt there. A couple of hundred years ago, folks used it to describe desperate men who had got themselves into the Navy to escape a pile of hurt they'd stacked for themselves on land. Some of these men joined up because they couldn't afford to feed themselves; they thought the Navy would give them a few meals and some shelter for their enlisting. For such men, the Navy and the waves were the last quarter.

Like those desperate men, the sick of Coral Point took to the sea in a final attempt at curing their ills. Or so some of the old timers thought. My thinking was that Graham took them out deep, so the fish and the brine could hide a bit of what he'd done to them.

Still, they usually floated up.

But Morris Planke had been found beneath his wine racks and a couple of kids had been found hiding in their closets as the crud took the last of their lives.

So, walking on toward Graham's slip, I started to feel a hint of normal coming back into my head, when I saw the aerials of his ninety-four foot Sunseeker. That name's a bit of a laugh, when you think about it, but Lord what a beautiful craft. Graham hadn't sailed off, and that gave me a bit of hope. But it didn't last.

Even before I could appreciate the yacht's fine lines, the teak decks and stainless steel railings, I noticed the gulls covering the flybridge, the bow and the aft deck. The flock was thick; a couple of the birds fluttered their wings as if threatening to desert the infested boat, but none flew away. A crowd of tourists wearing white pants, bright coloured tops, sunglasses and expressions of amused confusion had gathered on the dock to observe this odd congregation of seafowl. The tourists whispered to each other and pointed at the birds blanketing the vessel. Maybe they noticed, maybe they didn't, but every single one of those birds was facing west.

I walked on home, away from the tourists and the flock of scavenger birds that had gathered as if in mourning for an elder statesman, and I thought a good bit about my wife –

God rest her soul. Thinking about Graham invariably made me think about Judy.

She had been my wife for over fifteen years before she passed on. Judy was a good woman, but she'd been troubled and tortured by things I could never even imagine, and she'd numbed those difficulties with too much alcohol, particularly in those later years after her famous father had died.

I thought about Judy and I thought about Graham, and I didn't feel quite so at home in Coral Point anymore. The place was going bad, like that banker Bentley told me. You could smell it, and though it was easy enough to tell yourself that you were just getting a whiff of a landed thatch of seaweed, you knew that the scent wasn't drifting over the town, it was rising from it.

I never thought anything could be worse than that stink. Seaweed has about the nastiest stench the sea can produce. Judy always said it smelled like the inside of a dead whale's backside, and I figured that was about right.

She always had a funny way of looking at things, of saying things, and I imagine a lot of that came from her father. He'd been a writer from out of Louisiana; a little town called Marchand, up north near Shreveport. He wrote thick books (most of which I couldn't make it halfway through). One time, he'd brought his daughter on a trip to Coral Point to research one of those big books, and the old man and I got pretty close. Judy and I got closer.

I imagine she wanted a different kind of fellow than those that her father wanted for her. She used to laugh about the narrow, sleek men who surrounded her in Marchand. They were practical and book smart and just bored the life out of her. Now, I'm no prize, wasn't one back then. But Judy said she thought I was romantic, and I

14

think I misunderstood the way she meant the word, because I hadn't read a line of poetry.

Maybe she thought my superstitions were interesting. There are a lot of superstitions built by the sea, and she might have seen those as a bit romantic. Maybe she was right. After all, what are superstitions but a romantic way to look at fear?

Judy had deserved better than I could give her, but she never complained. When her father died, shot by a gang of kids in New York the night he had accepted some award for the big book he had written about the steel industry, Judy just kind of went quiet. They hadn't seemed terribly close for a lot of years, but that was natural enough. Still, after we got back from the funeral in Louisiana, she just went real quiet.

And she drank, maybe looking for a message in those bottles. If she ever found one, I never knew. Even after the doctors had told her about the diabetes, she kept on with the wine and the vodka. One day, her body just couldn't take any more, and she suffered a stroke that about killed her.

That might have been the kindest thing.

Instead she lingered, nothing but a mumbling shell, prone to tears and headaches that made her faint dead away from the pain. For two years, I tended to her until I thought that I might just give out from the strain of it all.

That night, with Graham's boat and the carrion funeral taking place on its decks behind me, the evening news out of Miami had a report about Morris Planke's death. The plastic-haired anchorman gave a brief tribute to the entrepreneur and mentioned a couple of his charitable acts amid a list of his successful businesses, including the hotel in Coral Point. They said he had succumbed to the flu and warned folks to get their flu shots, especially the young and the elderly and those who had existing medical conditions.

Flu shots wouldn't help. The tiny plague was over, but something worse was coming; that much was certain.

I can't say that I was terribly hungry that evening, but I do remember that I was chewing on a sandwich when the call came through for a morning charter.

Immediately, I declined the offer. The man on the other end of the phone swore a lot and wondered why he couldn't find a single damned boat captain in a town full of them. I suggested he try Bob Dickinson and listed a few other names, but the charter told me that those folks were already booked up solid. He offered me a few extra bucks, and I did a little math.

He seemed annoyed when I told him that I'd be willing to take his family out, but it would have to be after sunrise. He wanted to get an early start before all the marlin were snatched up, like the water had only so many to give, but I held firm. We could sail at sunrise, but not one damned minute before. He must have sensed that he had no choice, and that I wasn't going to budge on this point, so we set a time and a price.

Unfortunately, sailing at sunrise meant getting to the boat before sunrise.

2

Awake, with the sun still a good distance out over the Atlantic but moving my way, I made myself some strong coffee and filled a mug, lightening it with a couple of drops of condensed milk, the way I'd always taken it in the Navy. I dressed, packed myself a lunch and thermosed the rest of the coffee before heading out to meet my charter.

Coral Point, the town itself, was still quiet in the dull morning darkness.

Like most of the towns in the Keys, there's not much to Coral Point, not much at all, but it's got everything you need to get through the days. The main street, Dolphin, is lined with little shops and restaurants that don't put enough food on the plate to feed a good-sized snail, but I suppose the tourists liked them well enough, because during the season, those places were always full up.

Running parallel with Dolphin was Seabreeze, and that was the real town of Coral Point. Along Seabreeze, May and Ernie Ledford ran the supermarket and Doreen Nelson had a fine doughnut shop that sold the best jelly-filleds I ever tasted. Further down Seabreeze, close to the marina, Pete Scoggins ran a good hardware business

17

right across the street from Ethel's Luncheonette.

Most everything I'd need was already stored away on the *Judy Anne*. Reinaldo would be out early, and if he hadn't already shipped out with one of the other captains, I could buy whatever bait the charter needed from him. If he had, Tess over at the shop would have a good supply.

But I didn't see Reinaldo, and I didn't see Tess. I walked along the waterfront, and while I noticed about a dozen of the captains had already set out for the day, leaving empty slips like vacant, watery lots along the marina, I also noticed that the bustle that should have brought the planks alive in the dim, pre-dawn light was strangely absent.

Tess had not opened the bait shop. The storefront window, draped in green netting and decorated with an assortment of cheap reels and rods, was dark. I cupped my hands and put my face to the glass, but nothing moved inside, and my belly started to knot. The sea to my back lapped at the pylons and the pier, knocked hulls against their bumpers. I was surrounded by sounds, but they were the kind of desolate sounds that made you know you were alone. My boots clacked too loudly on the dock, and I tried to quiet my steps and, at the same time, move faster.

Those desolate sounds will get to you; they certainly worked their way under my skin. Even if I hadn't known about Graham and what remained in his wake, being out on those boards with the dark shops to my back and the rocking shadows of the boats ahead of me, all playing against those lonely sounds, would have been unsettling in itself.

Boats weren't meant to exist outside the context of human beings; they weren't meant to be alone. When they

18

were, they seemed the saddest, most mournful things, because they were, in their own way, living. Cars and planes and the like were just objects; they didn't move without man's interference; they sat like small shelters, immobile and just a part of the landscape. But when a boat is abandoned in its slip, it creaks with the cry of a frightened child, it rocks as if trembling with anticipation or fear, and it rolls up on the waves, as if searching the land for its captain.

I nearly didn't see Morris Planke, because of an odd need to be with my *Judy Anne*. Despite the morning gloom, I was aware of movement far down the dock, near Graham's lonely Sunseeker. Like a sail that had torn free of its mast, a flash of white fluttered over the boards against the plum purple horizon. The disturbance in my vision was quickly gone, and I figured that I'd just imagined the motion.

But then, it happened again. The flutter of white drew my eyes to the dock and the man standing there.

Like a ghost, dishevelled and drawn by the act of dying, Morris Planke stood twenty feet from me. He wore a white sheet around his shoulders, and his silver hair jutted out in every direction like he'd just been woken. The man who had owned the most expensive hotel in the Florida Keys, the man who had taken sick and had nearly 'scared the shit' out of a fat banker named Bentley, the man who had died early the previous morning, faced me on the empty pier.

Cold, as if the seawater were seeping through my pores, I dropped my canvas sack. It hit the boards with a dull thud. Planke's head bobbed with the motion, like a rooster pecking at the ground for a grub. When his black eyes, void of life and sense, locked back on mine, I caught a moment

19

of his fury. He charged forward; the sheet flapped behind him like a cape; his bare feet slapped the boards with each heavy step; his wild hair, rustling with the currents of wind, made him look insane, but he was beyond such common definitions.

Five feet before the old man would collide with my chest, he took to the air, leaping at the morning gloom and holding on as he rose over my head. I fell back, following his progress with my eyes and, at the same time, covering my face as I dropped onto the boards with a crash just like my canvas sack had.

I rolled over and saw the snapping white sheet in the purple air. Morris hung there, throwing glances downward at me and then to the west, seeming to weigh me against what he saw in the distance. Fortunately, escape was the old man's priority.

The sheet cracked in the air like the report of a small pistol, and the man sailed over the marina toward the gulf.

Two darker, smaller shapes waited in the air over the black waters to the west. When the flapping white sheet trailing behind Morris Planke broke the sky between them, the three glided out over the sea, away from the rising sun.

And I knew they were going in deep, maybe out past the reef. I got to my feet, trembling and searching desperately for any other living person, so I wouldn't have to be alone with the water and the dark morning and the orphaned boats.

3

After seeing Old Morris Planke, I completely forgot about the charter. I went on home and kept myself in the house. It wasn't the bravest thing to do, I'll admit, but a lot of fears, some fresh and others frayed by time, whistled around in my head, and they put me on edge. Even during full daylight, I got the jim-jams something awful. Memories of my Judy came back strong, and my head was like a cabinet that hadn't been secured before hitting rough waters, so everything jangled, shifted, spilled out and got mixed up together.

You see, I'd been there before.

For all of the dread of seeing Morris Planke running along that dock at me, it wasn't a unique experience. I'd seen his kind before, and it's never easy on civilized folks when they see something that feral.

It took me some time, a few days at least, to get my gear organised and reshelved in my head; but before that happened, some miserable dreams came my way. Maybe they weren't dreams exactly. In truth, I don't remember what played in my head when I was sleeping. It was the dreams I had when I was awake that threw me.

Now, these weren't delusions or hallucinations or any of that craziness; they were just memories and the darker interpretations of memories, crowding in to get my attention. Seeing Planke had put a little hole in my mind, and all these haunts were just the bilge pouring in.

A memory of my father came back to me, a strong and ugly memory. We were in a storm; we'd gone too far out. I was in the captain's cabin, and my father was on the deck, helping a man named Lars. Hungry faces appeared around them, rising up from the waves. The faces were of people I'd known from town, the victims of Graham's sickness. It was all mixed up in my head, and most of it didn't make any sense, but one of those dreams stuck with me. Naturally, my Judy was in it. The worst, most awful moments, just like the most wonderful, always include someone you love.

But like I said, I wasn't asleep. My eyes were open, and I lay in bed, looking at the window and seeing the morning light rise up on the glass. Judy sat in her wheelchair by the window, her head cocked to the side, her mouth twisted from the stroke. She looked at me and tried to speak; half her mouth opened and closed like she was chewing. Her hair rose from her stricken face in broad black ribbons, like kelp caught in a gentle current, and I realised that she was in my room, in her chair, but she was also in the water. She was down deep. Her gown rippled with the insistent tide that worked around her and under her.

The water carried her up, out of the chair, toward the ceiling. Her head turned toward the window and her hair swam around her. Seeing the morning light creeping over the sill, she jerked away from the glass as if yanked by a diving line.

I sat up in the bed and tried to shake the image from my

head, but motion only made it worse, somehow clearer. I saw every line in Judy's face, every red vein in her eyes. A bubble of air had latched at the corner of her mouth, and I so badly wanted to reach out and wipe it away.

Lord help me, I wanted it all wiped away.

After about four days – it may have been five, I don't exactly remember – I got up to put on the coffee and realised that the tin was empty. Unlike the previous mornings, sweat hadn't pasted me to the sheets, and Judy's ghost – that gift of my imagination – wasn't drifting in the imagined currents of my room. Instead, I felt rested and stronger, like my kit was secured again, so I made myself presentable – shaved and showered. I did a quick inventory of the cupboards and the Frigidaire and set out to the grocery store.

Sawyer's Market wasn't much of a store by city standards, but it had everything most folks could need. The shelves were neatly stacked and evenly spaced under bars of fluorescent lights. A handful of people, mostly familiar to me, were pushing small shopping carts in the aisles, filling them up like they did before a big storm came through. Bitsy Hoffman gave me a solemn look over the four boxes of Hamburger Helper she had clutched to her chest, and I nodded a greeting. About a week had passed since Bitsy's nephew had been found dead of the sickness, and my heart went out to that whole family.

I hate to see suffering. Just plain hate it. It makes me stomach-sick and bad-brained, and I don't want to have a single thing to do with it. That's why I stopped the commercial fishing so many years ago. It wasn't a matter of guilt or anything foolish like that. I mean, those fish that we caught were going to feed people; they weren't going to be wasted, and that's a fine thing. But when I looked at those creatures, yanked from their natural place and spilled out on a deck – their mouths working furiously to get a little more water over their gills; their bodies flopping on the wet wood – it just got to me after a time.

I said, 'Morning,' to Bitsy and tried to give her a warm smile, but it just didn't feel right.

She tried nodding her head and clipped her chin on a box of Hamburger Helper. Then, she bent over her cart and piled the packages on her other groceries and wheeled the cart away.

Over by the milk, I saw Horatio Stocks. Stocks was a burly young man with a few days of black stubble on his chin and a pair of jeans that were wrinkled so bad they looked like they had been wadded up for a month. He was Doc Davis's assistant. I guess I knew Horatio well enough, and I should have said good morning to him, but he also had himself a damned low face. I turned my cart down the aisle before he noticed me, because he had that suffering look, and I imagined he too had lost someone close to him.

In my haste to get out of Horatio's line of sight, I all but ran down a slight woman in a pair of khakis who seemed very interested in a can of pears.

Claire Smith was her name, and she was a delicate, attractive woman who owned a dress shop over on Dolphin Avenue. Her husband had run off a few years back with a singer from New Orleans and had taken a good chunk of Claire's family money with him, but she was doing fine, all things considered. I'd known her for about as long as I could remember, but we'd never said more than a word or two to each other in passing.

24

She was a member of our small city council, but when I'd gone to speak to them the day after noticing that Graham had returned to Coral Point, she'd been out of town, visiting her sister in Port St Lucie. Considering how that meeting had gone, I imagined it was better she hadn't attended.

Looking up from her can of pears, she said, 'I have no idea if I should be eating these or not.'

Maybe it was the confusion of the last few days, or it might just have been the fact that she was speaking to me in such a friendly way, but I found my guts all tied up and tingling, like I was a little boy asking her out for a soda.

'I'd imagine they're pretty good for you,' I finally said.

'Well, yes. You'd think so, but they're swimming around in that heavy syrup. That can't be good for you.'

'Tastes good, though.'

Claire looked over her shoulder, down the aisle, as if searching for prying ears. She leaned close to me and whispered, 'The syrup's my favourite part. I don't even really care much for the pears.'

That got me to smiling, and I was so surprised at the good feeling in my chest that I laughed out loud. Claire giggled, and she looked just as fine as frog's hair. I always thought she was a looker. Sometimes, I walked by her shop on Dolphin just to get an eyeful of her, but her standing in that grocery aisle, grinning and holding the can of fruit, made her seem more real to me, more like a person I could spend time with.

At that moment, Bitsy Hoffman pushed her cart across the mouth of the aisle; her mournful expression turned sharp and bitter, like she was appalled that anyone might ever laugh again now that her nephew was dead. Claire's face burned red, and she dropped her head, until Bitsy disappeared behind a display of paper towels.

'That poor woman,' Claire said, all shame and hurt. 'Between little Edward's death and Doc Davis, it's a wonder she can find the strength to get out of bed.'

'Doc Davis?' I asked. I didn't know what might have happened to the man, but I thought about the sad face of his assistant, Horatio, and I imagined it couldn't be good.

'He up and left a few days ago,' Claire told me. 'Didn't leave a note or a message or anything. He and Bitsy have been seeing each other for a good year now, and she went over to his house the other morning. Doc didn't answer. Nobody's seen him. Even Horatio doesn't know where he got off to.'

In my head, Morris Planke, dressed in a white sheet, raced over a dark pier, his bare feet slapping the boards, his white hair jutting in tangles before he took to the air.

You see, Doc Davis pulled double duty in Coral Point; he had his own family practice and served a good number of the families in town, but he also worked as the medical examiner. The bodies they found would be taken to his office, and he would be the last one to see them before Lester Coombs took them on over to the mortuary.

'We can all hope he comes back soon,' Claire said, putting the can of pears in her cart. She plucked another off the shelf, flashed me a guilty smile and set it next to the other. 'Maybe they'll make me feel better.'

'Maybe they will,' I said. Then I excused myself, turned away and finished my shopping.

The next day, a scuba diver by the name of Roger

Washington disappeared during an afternoon dive out past the reef. His diving buddy, a guy named Mike Sterns, was rushed to the hospital with the bends.

A heart attack killed him later that night.

4

The sun was high and baked the docks with mid-afternoon heat. Calm water, as blue as you could wish for, lapped at the pilings and barely influenced even the smaller boats. Graham's yacht, the ninety-foot Sunseeker, didn't move at all. The gulls had cleared off her decks, their respects paid. Few people wandered the docks. The season was about to begin in earnest, and the marina was as quiet as Christmas. Hard times were coming, but we'd all been through those before. A good storm could eat up a half-year's profit before it played out.

But this was a gale that wouldn't pass, not unless something was done, and the only hope I could find for myself and my home was Graham. He had brought this misery to Coral Point. If he was still alive, he could put a stop to it. If he was dead, and I believed he was, then there wasn't a damned thing to be done.

So, I stood on the waterfront, feeling safe and comfortable under the daylight and not wanting to trade it for the shadow inside Graham's shelter, when I saw Tim Planke standing down the way by a good-sized Hunter sailboat.

He wore sunglasses and a white polo shirt that draped over his paunch. A nasty look was carved on his face, but that was nothing new. He was the sorriest piece of wealth I'd ever met, and I didn't have much time for folks like that.

But the thing was, even from that distance, I could see him scowling at me. Not just wearing his spoiled brat expression out of a general disgust for the world, but focusing that distaste on me, like I'd stolen his girl or spread some secret he'd have rather kept quiet. And it occurred to me that only a week or so before, I'd faced his father on this same pier.

Tim Planke shoved his hands in the pockets of his navy blue shorts, pulling his shirt tight over his substantial belly. He did a quick, nervous jig, as if not certain which way to walk, and then he turned around and left the dock.

I looked at Graham's boat, so peaceful in its mooring, cast another glance back at the sailboat and then went aboard.

Though shadowed by the smoked glass windows, the main saloon of Graham's yacht was something of a wonder. I'd spent a lot of time on boats in my day: battleships and fishing rigs and speedboats – even a few sailing ships. You get used to a level of discomfort and dreariness when you're out for long stretches, and after a while it feels just as fine as home. But this vessel was something different.

I stepped into a living room, bigger than the one I had at home, with curved, black leather couches built into the port and starboard sides and facing off on one another across the cabin. Crystal light fixtures, shaped like long tulips, clutched the wall above them. Further in, I found a mahogany dining table, set for six with plenty of space between the chairs. Candlesticks, affixed to the tabletop, wore caps of melted wax.

At the spiral staircase that corkscrewed down, deeper into the craft, I turned a wall switch, but the darkness kept hold. Either Graham had removed the lights, or his rig had been sitting too long and the juice had died. I'd come prepared and pulled a flashlight from my pocket, tested it on the wall and took my first step toward the shadows.

The lower deck was pitch dark; even the portholes had been covered. My little flashlight cut a sharp but slim path through the air, and I thought about Roger Washington, that scuba diver who had disappeared out past the reef. He would have carried a dive light with him, something powerful to cut the gloom, like one of those fancy light cannons. I imagined him deep in the water, snaking through one of the wrecks, his light's beam showing only a narrow corridor through the black ocean. He would have seen the rusted hull and anything that remained intact from the wreck – the berths and tables, maybe a personal photograph tacked to the wall by a sailor, now wet and ruined and littering the floor.

Then, Morris Planke's vicious and dead-weathered face would have risen up in his narrow shaft of light.

Standing on the lower deck of Graham's yacht, my neck cold-pimpled, and I swung my flashlight from one wall to the next, fully expecting Morris Planke to be charging down the hall toward me. Of course, Morris was not there.

I found a fine stateroom, with a quilted duvet made of a golden fabric; there was a small crew's quarters; and at the bow, another large cabin with a bed and attached head.

The smell had been on me since I stepped onto this deck; it was a familiar odour. My Judy would have called it the backside-of-a-whale stench, but I knew that it wasn't landed weeds. This rotten smell had come not from the ocean but from land, and since I'd found nothing on that deck, I figured the source was below.

Another spiralling set of stairs twisted down. The odour was stronger here, and I thought it might be better to leave. I believe that Nature knew what she was doing when she designed pungency in death; it was a warning to folks that something bad had happened, and they should steer damned well clear of it.

Steering clear would have been just fine with me, but a lot of badness was waiting outside once night fell. I had to know if Graham was in any condition to stop it.

In my head, Morris Planke followed me down that black hallway. I kept the light steady, but my nerves were dancing like gnats at a light bulb. Every moment was the one just before his clawed old hands fell on me. And Judy was there too.

Opening an aft cabin door, I saw her floating. Her lips rippled and chewed, trying to speak words. The lone bubble of air still clung to the corner of her mouth. Her eyes were closed, but she saw me. I felt certain of that.

I put the memory of my wife behind me, hurried down the corridor and found Graham in the forward stateroom. He was dead, or rather death had taken him on permanently.

Part of me was grateful that he was gone. Though he had commanded more than a little of my respect over the years, and I knew Coral Point was well and truly cursed without him, I was damned glad to see him dead.

But he hadn't gone quietly, and he hadn't died alone.

31

My flashlight beam ran over the contents of the room, exposing snapshot fragments. A bed took up most of the cabin's space, with narrow aisles on either side. The aisle between the bed and an upholstered bench led back to the head. Graham lay face up in this aisle; thick chunks of wood, like breach plugs, jutted from his chest and belly. His face looked just as it had the last time I'd seen him. Not handsome but far from ugly, he was a man who had fitted in at yacht club dances and at dockside bars, depending on which clothes he had chosen to wear.

He had a barrelled chest and a square, rugged face with a thick moustache. The corks of wood – five in all – nested in the hair on his chest and the smooth white skin of his belly. No blood seeped from his wounds.

But there was blood in the cabin.

It was all over the walls, and a fan of it sprayed the white comforter, which had been crumpled and wadded at the bed's edge.

Part of a man lay sideways against the headboard.

He had been torn in two. His torso ended just above the navel, and a knobbed tail – the bottom of his spine – rested in a pool of blood and bile and filth. My belly rose high into my throat as the light played over this horror. I bit down hard on the sick and pushed it low, back into my gut.

Something moved on the deck above me – a footstep that just about stopped my heart. I froze in place with my light's beam on the face of the torn man. A dark beard clutched his jaw line; the skin above it was stark and ashen.

I knew him.

Another footstep above, and I backed out of the cabin, quietly closed the door and retreated down the hall to hide in the lower saloon until I knew who else had dared to board Graham's cursed vessel. I had just taken my position by the wall when light bathed the twisted stairway. A black leg came into view and then caught a taste of the beam so I could tell that this intruder wore wrinkled denim jeans.

Horatio Stocks screamed when I said, 'Hello.'

'That was Cole Westman,' Horatio said, once we'd traded the pit of Graham's boat for the afternoon light on the pier. The sun felt like a cleansing shower on my face and neck; it helped wash away some of the dread I'd collected below. I'd let Horatio give the room a good examination, because he knew what to look for when it came to dead folks, but he didn't tell me anything I didn't already know. Graham had been attacked in his sleep, and though he'd been fast enough to make bait out of Cole Westman, he had ultimately been outmanned, which meant that others, maybe several others, had been in that room.

Horatio's upper lip twitched under his stubble. He looked stricken and exhausted, and for the second time he said, 'That was Cole.'

I understood his disbelief. Cole Westman was a bull of a man who looked like he could bench press a bus. Over the years, Cole had gotten into a lot of trouble, mostly just brawling down at Tib's when he'd had one beer too many. Understanding the benefits of muscle, Tim Planke had hired Cole to manage marina security a half a dozen years back, and he'd cut an impressive figure, barking instructions to his crew and berating the snow birds who wore their inexperience like vivid Hawaiian shirts. Cole had mellowed a bit, taking great pride in his position at the marina, but no-one forgot his ability to do damage to anyone who flipped the switch on his temper.

And there he had been, opened up and discarded on the bed in Graham's stateroom.

'We better call the Sheriff,' Horatio muttered. His lip continued its rapid dance.

'Don't bother,' I told him. Horatio gave me a confused, sad-dog look. 'There's nothing he can do about this.'

'That's what Doc Davis said.'

Horatio's words stopped me cold. I assumed Doc Davis had gotten himself killed, drained out by Morris Planke or one of them kids.

'I don't follow,' I said.

'He called a couple of days after he left town. Wouldn't tell me where he'd gone, but he told me to grab everyone I loved and get my ass out of Coral Point. He was talking crazy shit. Evil-this and evil-that. He said something about Old Morris and Bitsy Hoffman's nephew, but it didn't make any sense. So, I asked him if he'd told the Sheriff, and he said what you just said.'

I clapped Horatio on the shoulder, trying to give him a bit of support, because he had worked himself into a froth over all this. I wish I had been able to think of something to help calm him, but I was only a few thrashes away from a froth myself, so I said, 'You better do what the Doc told you.'

Of course that wasn't what Horatio Stocks wanted to hear, but I couldn't help that. Truth was, there wasn't a damned thing any of us could do.

Graham had been a smart bastard. The ones that had died, the ones that had turned, would have been fragile folks in life – the elderly or the young. He'd harvested those types in case he didn't get around to draining them all. Those that turned, being frail in their human state, would be relatively weak until they matured, making them

34

easy for Graham to dispose of after the harvest.

Needless to say, Graham wasn't likely to be helping us any time soon.

Horatio stood before me – still shaking, still confused. There was nothing left for me to say on the matter (certainly nothing that would comfort him), so I walked away. I looked to the horizon, where the sun burned close to the water.

I went home and locked the doors. There was nothing else to be done.

5

'I'm not saying that I won't help you; I'm telling you that I *can't* help you.'

My words hung in the air as palpable as the thin haze of cigarette smoke filling the bar; my admission of impotence just floated there waiting to be snatched up by one of the three people, two men and a woman, who faced me across the scarred and stained tabletop. The three big shots from town looked at me as if they didn't understand the plain English I was speaking, but with this kind of people, if they weren't hearing what they wanted to hear, their ears just stopped working.

Three weeks had passed since I'd encountered Old Morris Planke on the dock to watch him fly off into the pre-dawn sky, flanked by two children who had also succumbed to Graham's infection. Since then, at least one more child and three more adults had been found, curled up in the dark places of their homes, dead from the crud but not quite ready for death. A good dozen folks had been reported missing at sea since then, and though a few of us knew what was happening to these unfortunate souls, there wasn't really anything to be done about it.

My three guests didn't quite see it that way.

But these were the worst kind of people, desperate, frightened people, who simply didn't understand the sheer depths of their troubles.

We were sitting in *El Tiburón*, a waterfront bar with the smell of the sea and those who worked her etched as finely into the panelled walls and plank bar as the image of Neptune was etched into the column by the head. At late afternoon, with a full sun in the sky, Tib's main room was thick with gloom. The bar's nautical theme, the nets and lanterns (a bit of a slap to those of us who had actually made our living on the water), had grown on me over the years.

The three people, the desperate and frightened ones, sat at my table, looking like they'd just fallen off the deck of a yacht and onto a derelict barge. We'd all grown up in Coral Point, but if the city had had railroad tracks, we'd have lived on different sides of them. They didn't belong in Tib's any more than I belonged in their company, but there we were talking – and I have to believe it was English – and they still weren't understanding me.

'We'll triple your fee,' Claire Smith said. 'We have the money.'

'Then you might want to consider using it to take a vacation,' I told her. 'A long vacation.'

'We're wasting our time,' Tim Planke said. That man had always struck me as trouble. He had a six-foot chip on the shoulder of his five-and-a-half foot frame, and had those little, dark eyes, like a sand shark right before it goes for the meat of your calf in shallow water. 'He can't help us. He doesn't know shit.'

I thought about Cole Westman, then. How he'd been hired by Planke to do his dirty chores. How he'd been torn in two and discarded. The thought really scraped my craw.

'I know enough not to kill the goddamned thing before he harvests,' I said, showing just enough amusement to really piss the runt off.

Then the smart one, the man with the tweed and flannel, cautioned his friend. 'Now, hold on, Timothy,' Clyde Hoover said, with a calm professorial voice. 'We could help you,' Clyde said to me. 'We'll go with you.'

'Since I'm not going,' I told him, 'I find that hard to believe.'

'Don't you even care what happens?' Claire asked.

God but she was a good looking woman, and her voice, all innocent desperation, did go a ways to wake my conscience. But I wasn't going to be swayed by guilt, not even when it was dished up by such a charming lady. Of course, that didn't stop her from trying.

'You live here too,' she continued.

'He can't help us,' Planke snarled. 'He'd probably just take our money and high tail it to Key West, and we'd still be sitting here in the dark with our fingers up our asses.'

'You ever find anything interesting up there?' I asked, to get a rise out of the sawed-off jerk.

Planke made a move as if to rise, like he might come over the table at me. But it was just a show. Claire looked properly frightened, and the smart one, Clyde, leaned forward and put his tweed-covered arm out to keep his buddy's ass in the chair. I just kept smiling and lifted my mug, giving Planke a low salute before I drained the beer from her.

'As I see it, you've got a couple of choices,' I told them, and this got their interest. Well, it got Claire's and Clyde's interest. Planke remained slouched in his chair, sulking like a brat who had gotten the wrong colour pony for his birthday. And I almost decided to take the guy's advice and get my tail down to Key West – just leave the little prick with his problem. But that Claire was a nice woman, a good woman, and she deserved to know what she was up against, even if it didn't do her much good.

'You killed him before the harvest,' I began. Now, I know I said that before, but it was important, and it needed some repeating. 'It goes like this: he infects; he waits while they get sick; and then he harvests. Now, if he doesn't drain them before they die, then they turn.'

'No shit,' Planke mumbled.

'Timothy,' Claire warned. 'But these aren't like him.'

'That's right, they're not,' I said, as kindly as I could manage. Something about the woman reminded me of my Judy, so I wanted to be kind with her. I can't tell you how many years I'd had my eye on Claire; too many years to be holding such a flame for her to be sure, especially since I was keenly aware of the social fence that separated us, but I couldn't let that little fire burn out. If nothing else, it made me want to help, not through action but through explanation so she might understand the dark days to come. 'Graham was the real deal. Born and bred. There aren't many of those left, and they aren't as strong as you'd think. He needs to harvest, because plain old type-O is only going to get him so far. He infects, and the blood takes on some fuller body, takes on a form that can sustain him. And then he feeds and moves on. Graham knew better than to stay in one place too long. He docked for a few weeks, took his food and sailed off. But Graham was efficient; he cleaned up after himself. He never left any to turn behind him, at least none I ever heard of.'

'You admired him,' Clyde pointed out with some awe.

Damned right, I did. You admired your adversary or

you fed him; that's what I'd always believed. It didn't matter what kind of animal you hunted, you had to respect it and know it. You even had to love it a little, because if you don't love something, there ain't no way in hell you can kill it, unless you're completely rotten inside, like that snivelling Tim Planke. 'As I said, Graham was efficient.'

'No wonder you didn't stop him,' Planke scoffed.

'Well, sir,' I said to the little man, 'when I came to you last month, you threatened to have me arrested if I tried, because he was such a hit at your yacht club dances. It didn't matter that all those folks went down with the sickness. No sir, it didn't matter until your father got a vein full of his juice and started to get sick, then you were the first one on his boat with a crucifix and a stake.'

'Fucking crosses don't work,' Planke said. 'He could have killed me.'

I knew damned well the jerk hadn't been anywhere near Graham on the day of his death. He might have gone onto the boat to keep an eye out for curious tourists or locals, but the real work had been left up to Cole Westman and his buddies. People like Planke don't stick their necks out; they just pay other folks to lie on the block.

'He's not a devil or spirit,' I told him. And again, I said it in plain English. He seemed to be educated enough, but he also seemed dumb as a rudder. 'Religious symbolism wouldn't do a damned thing against him.'

'But what are *these* things?' Claire insisted; her voice real close to breaking. The sound of it just tore right through me, because Judy used to have that tone when I'd tell her I had to go out deep during the storm season.

'They're feeders,' I told her simply, not wanting to use any of the vulgar names I'd heard used for them over the years. 'The sickness that followed their infection wiped all the sense right out of them. They died as they were born, with nothing but hunger and some innate understanding of where to find their food. They hunt and they feed.'

'Just tell us how to kill them,' Planke said impatiently.

Have you ever met someone you just didn't like? I'd felt that way about the man since first setting eyes on him. He might have been the nicest, most generous fellow on the Earth, might have given me bottles of rum for Christmas, and I'd still just plain hate the sight of him.

'You want to know how to kill them?' I asked, clutching my mug real tight in my hand. 'Well, you picture yourself out on a boat, maybe that nice seventy-five footer of yours, out in the middle of the ocean with nothing around but water and mist and a few dolphin arcing by the bow. And remember it's night time, so dark your lights cut only a dozen yards in any direction. Then imagine six or seven of these things coming up from the waves or out of the skies, or both. They hit you like a school of piranha and don't pull their teeth out until you ain't got nothing in your veins but air.' I stared into my glass, because I felt real bad about the worry my words had put on Claire's face. 'You picture that,' I said to Planke, fixing him with a gaze that told him I wasn't fooling around. 'And you tell me how to kill them.'

'What about when they're sleeping?' Clyde asked.

I shook my head. Those scuba divers, Roger Washington and Mike Sterns, had probably come across the school while they were sleeping. It hadn't kept the two men alive.

'You won't get these when they're sleeping. They've gone in deep. They could be in one of a dozen wrecks sunk beyond the coral; they could hide in the caverns twenty fathoms down, or they might just rest on the bottom, so low the sun doesn't reach them. Now, you go into any of those places with a scuba outfit, and it's over, because they're going to move fast, faster than barracuda. And there ain't one of you that would have the strength to stake 'em that low. And save the James Bond crap about spear guns, because you haven't got the aim. You might get one, but that leaves a good school of 'em to finish you off. So, I'm going to say it again – use your money to get some distance from Coral Point. Or stay off the water at night.'

'And watch the town shrivel up and die?' Planke said.

'The town's survived hurricanes; it'll survive this,' I told him, and I didn't say it nasty like, because I wanted him to believe me. More than that, I *needed* Claire to believe me. 'They'll move on if they don't get fed. Or they'll come onto land, which will make killing them a little more likely.'

'And if they don't?' Planke challenged.

'Then they don't. But these schools don't last long out in the water, because the feeding is sporadic. They break apart and land themselves soon enough.' I didn't mention one school, a particularly vicious and intelligent school that – for all I knew, or cared to know – still hunted the waters thirty miles east of Key West. I'd seen them work before, while working a tuna boat with my father, still dreamed about it – terrible dreams those were, dark as hell and filled with demons.

Still, the crew of the *Maria Brava*, infected and left to die, was uncommon. Most feeders that went under the waves took to land when the benefits of living deep were outweighed by the scarcity of food.

'We have to do something,' Claire said, so sweetly it made the hair on my neck tingle. 'If you won't help us, then we'll have to do it ourselves.'

42

'And I wish you wouldn't do that,' I said, putting down my mug before standing from the table. 'Now, if you'll excuse me. It's getting late, and I've got a charter tomorrow. Good night.'

6

Truth was, I didn't have a charter the next morning, hadn't had a new charter in weeks, but I didn't want those folks, especially that Claire woman, talking me into anything like suicide. I'd lived a lot of years on the water, and the ocean had been good to me, but it had also taught me to survive. That's not to say that I'm afraid of death. Truth be told, death seems like a nice way to pass your time – no cuts from running line, no calluses and no muscle aches, just a nice relaxing nap. Who knows, maybe even some nice dreams. I imagine it's something like a comfortable bed at the end of a good day's work, but you've got to finish that day's work before you can lie down or you haven't earned the rest.

So, I lay awake for a couple of hours, remembering the three folks and thinking about Claire with her neat crop of brown hair and those nice blue eyes, and I hoped they took a little of what I'd told them to heart.

It was bad enough when a harvest was interrupted, leaving behind a couple of stragglers to make a mess before you brought them down, but to have a school of the things hunting together – well that was just plain evil. And when it happened, brother you didn't mess with them. You let them do their evil, and you hoped they moved on. Or, you moved on yourself, because the area they roamed was as good as poison.

The morning after was a dark day and felt just plain bad. Nature seemed to agree and had blown in some storm clouds to blot out the sun and cover the town in grey. A heavy chop and the threat of thunderstorms had kept most of the captains landed, their charters preferring an afternoon in their hotels or the houses they'd rented for the season. Normally, I would have kept myself at home and pretended to be useful, but the papers and the news reports were a questionable source of information. Days could pass before a small column of type mentioned the family from Baltimore that had disappeared while taking a moonlight picnic out by the reef or ran an obituary for a captain, like that Trevor Bunn who hadn't been seen in nearly a month since the night he set out to check his shrimp traps. If you wanted good information, and wanted it fast, you needed to get into town.

I checked the sky, figured the rain wouldn't be coming for another couple of hours, and set off for Ethel's.

The diner was filled with captains and mates; they looked worn and old; even the young ones had long faces and drooping shoulders as if they'd just docked from a few days of rough water. Mizzie scurried from one table to the next with coffee and plates, telling folks that Fred Milner, a captain who had been chartering off of Coral Point for as long as I had, finally floated ashore. His bloated body was found rolled up against the rocks not a quarter of a mile down the coast.

'And he was nibbled to the bone,' Mizzie told me, brandishing her information proudly as if it were an engagement ring for my appreciation. 'The fish nearly picked him clean. They had to identify him by his teeth,' she said. 'Some family was out hunting sea shells and the littlest girl, that poor dear, came across his head and a bit of spine that was still attached. Such a horrible thing for a child to see.'

I nodded, and Mizzie lit up like a beacon. She poured me a cup of coffee and then turned to observe the room, her happily-glowing face sweeping round like the beam from a lighthouse. Then, she leaned close, her shrub of red hair nearly brushing my nose, and whispered, 'They say that a few small crabs had already made a fine home in his skull. About scared the life out of one of the coast guards who was bagging his remains when one of the little nippers climbed out and clamped onto his thumb.'

Mizzie found this information funny, and she snorted a laugh that made me cold.

Before long, I had a pretty significant list of folks that we'd never see in Ethel's Luncheonette again. Some of the stories were speculation and some were just plain lies, but the fact remained that we'd never see Cole Westman, Roger Washington, Molly Gerston, Tip Wansley, Mike Tosch or Gerald Kennedy again, and the news just made me angry when I realised that those innocent folks hadn't needed to die, wouldn't have died, if it hadn't been for that damned Tim Planke.

Clyde Hoover came in a little after noon and walked right on over to my table like we had a lunch appointment. He dropped into the seat and adjusted his blue blazer; above the collar, his serious, hawk-sharp face locked me with an expression of warm interest like he was trying to console me at a funeral or some such nonsense.

'I know why you won't help us,' Clyde said quietly,

46

keeping his voice low as Mizzie scurried our way. Mizzie took Clyde's order for coffee and, sensing that she had interrupted a conversation she wanted to hear, lingered over the table, waiting for the discussion to resume.

'Can I help you?' Clyde asked Mizzie, his voice too haughty for his surroundings.

'Just writing down the order,' Mizzie said, even as her cheeks began to pulse with crimson embarrassment.

'C-o-f-f-e-e,' Clyde said. 'It can't take much longer than that to write it down.'

Mizzie turned to walk back to the counter, looking hurt and shamed. 'She's got feelings,' I pointed out. 'Even if she doesn't belong to your yacht club.'

Clyde pretended he didn't hear me; he leaned on the table and whispered: 'This is about your wife, isn't it?'

'That's none of your business.'

'Ha,' Clyde said, as if he'd just won a prize by knocking over milk bottles at a carnival. 'I knew it. When you wouldn't help us last night, I did some digging, and found out that Judy died of the sickness four years ago.'

'It was in the papers,' I told him, to let him know that he hadn't uncovered any tremendous secret.

'Graham infected her,' Clyde continued. 'That's how you knew what was going to happen; you went through this the last time he docked here.'

Mizzie returned with the coffee; she eyed us both with the intensity of a gull on a grunion; she set Clyde's cup down and then, catching a hot look from his eyes, hurried back to chat with a booth full of boatsmen.

'Why didn't you just kill him when you saw that he'd come back?' Clyde asked. 'Why did you come to us for permission? You had to know we wouldn't believe you.'

'That's right,' I said. 'And I didn't particularly want

to spend the rest of my life in prison. I'm not Tim Planke; Sheriff Unger is not a buddy of mine who might turn the other way. So, I thought if you folks knew why Graham had to die, you'd see to it that nobody looked too deeply into the matter.'

'Well, we certainly believe you now.'

'And it's too late to do anything about it.'

'How do you know so much about him?' Clyde asked.

This was where I felt it necessary to lie. Clyde Hoover didn't need to know the real story, the truth that swirled around the death of my Judy, he just needed something he could believe in to fill the holes in his investigation. So I gave him that.

'Graham buddied up with me one night at Tib's. He walked in, just like you did a few minutes ago, and came right on over to my table. He was an elegant gentleman, and when he approached me, I imagined he was looking for a boat captain to hire, so I didn't think much about it at first. But as we talked, I found out about his Sunseeker and the way he lived, docking here and there and shipping out a few weeks later, and I knew he didn't need me to show him the water; he knew it better than I ever would.

'Well, we must have talked for a good two hours, and I invited him out to the house for dinner one night while he was in Coral Point. Just being polite, because I didn't imagine a gentleman of his stature would have much interest in sharing gumbo or dolphin with me and Judy.

'But he accepted the offer.'

Clyde sipped his coffee, eyeing me with a bit of suspicion, and that was fine, because I was lying after all. I was doing a decent job of it, but I had to expect a little disbelief on the part of a man who had about fifty college

48

degrees that he'd never have to use because of his family's oil interests.

'I keep thinking that maybe he made me ask him to dinner. Sometimes they can do that sort of thing. It's subtle and they can't make you do much damage, but they can get you to think along their lines. Anyway, he came to dinner.

'That's when he told me that he'd be in town for only a couple more weeks before setting out to Nassau. He told me that he always picked up a crew of Haitians down there; they were often displaced and worked cheap and proved excellent in helping him captain the boat to the Pacific and then Asia and so on until he had made it around the globe. Years ago, he had settled into a pattern of travel that suited him, and every four years or so, he found himself in Coral Point.'

'And that's when he infected your wife?' Clyde asked, cool yet eager for an answer.

'A few days after that dinner, Judy came down with the crud. I didn't want to believe she was parish damned like the others, but a week later, she went missing. That's when I knew about Graham. I went out to his mooring, but the big yacht was gone. Tess told me that he'd shipped out in the middle of the night, probably on his way down to Nassau.

'I could have killed him then,' I said. 'I wanted to kill him then, and I wouldn't have cared about going to jail, but he'd gotten out to sea and I knew I'd never track him down.

'Judy washed up the next day.'

'I'm sorry,' Clyde said. And you know, I believed him. He seemed genuinely hurt by my loss, and that made me adjust my opinion of the educated man, who had been rude to Mizzie and who had aligned himself with a fellow like Tim Planke. Clyde wasn't a bad guy; he was just rich, and that meant I couldn't understand him so well.

I thanked him for his concern.

'So you found out everything you could about them,' he went on, real eager like a kid who wants to know what happens to a princess in a fairy tale. 'You made them your field of study.'

'Something like that.'

Actually, I'd known about Graham and his kind for most of my life, but there was no reason to bring that up. Clyde had what he needed, and since I'd already lied a lot more than was comfortable, I thought it best to get out from under the subject.

'And you really believe there's nothing we can do?' Clyde asked.

'Yes,' I replied. 'I believe there's nothing you can do.'

'And there's nothing we can say to get you to help us?'

'There is no way I'm going out to the reef or anywhere else on the water at night. Not anymore.'

7

On Dolphin Street, standing in front of an ice cream parlour called Marbles, I rolled some of what that Clyde had said around in my head, and felt a bit out of sorts. He'd done a lot of looking at the road I'd travelled, and it struck me as rude of him. He had no right bringing my Judy into his troubles, no matter how good he thought his reasons were.

The street around me was a bit too quiet for my tastes. I'd hoped a little bustle would be distracting. Normally this time of year, the sidewalks were packed with shoppers in bright shirts and dark glasses, pointing at window displays and carrying bags full of clothes, or souvenirs or doo-dahs from one of the fancy craft stores. A small cluster of tourists had gathered on the next block, chatting and looking perplexed. I had no business on Dolphin Street exactly, I was just feeling a little down and wasn't quite ready for home. So, I'd taken a stroll and hoped to find a few friendly faces, but everyone I saw looked dragged out or just plain lost, like those tourists down the way.

I wandered down a few shop fronts, stopped in front of

a window that separated two mannequins – all done up in light, gauzy summer clothes – and looked inside. Through the display glass, I saw Claire's nice brown hair bobbing behind a rack of clothes.

Then, she rose up a few inches, and I saw her brow. A second later, more of her face appeared, and my heart froze. She seemed to be floating into the air above the rack of dresses, just as my Judy had floated in all those morning daydreams.

But Claire wasn't floating; she was climbing a ladder, carrying a hat that she placed on a plastic head, which sat high on a shelf. After adjusting the brim and cocking the hat just a bit to the left, she turned and saw me at the window.

I tried to smile and lifted a hand to wave, but the look on her face took all the energy right out of me. If she had been angry, I might have shrugged it off and put it down to just another wealthy fool, pouting about not getting her way, but the look she gave me was just a heart breaker.

I'd disappointed her. I could see that in the set of her mouth and the weight in her eyes. That look just gouged at my chest and followed me all the way home.

The last time I saw my Judy alive, she was sitting in her wheelchair, facing the window and mumbling at the glass. I'd just woken; it was the middle of the night and moonlight bathed her with a terrible grey glow. Her mouth moved in that chewing way; her head sagged to one shoulder; the crud's red blotches ran from her brow down the right side of her face, over her neck and into the collar of her nightgown. Sweat covered her face and darkened the fabric covering her breasts. Seeing her there by the window, suffering the way she was, I asked if she needed anything, knowing she couldn't answer.

But then it struck me just how wrong this was. When I'd gone to sleep, she'd been next to me in the bed; I'd put her there hours before. The chair was by the window where I kept it, but how had she gotten across the room?

I moved to get up, but couldn't. My legs felt like they'd been cast in cement. I called from the bed, already knowing these would be our last moments together. She'd been sick with the crud for over a week, so I knew the water would be calling her soon enough. I don't remember all the things I said, but I told my Judy how much I loved her and how wonderful she'd made my life and that her suffering was nearly done.

Her lips kept moving, but the sounds pushing at them were the incomprehensible gurglings of a child. I tried to get up, wanted to hold her one last time, but the last arms she felt around her wouldn't be mine.

Graham was in the room with us, had been the whole time. He stepped out of the shadows and walked over to the chair where my Judy waited. His square, rugged face hovered over her while he petted her hair and looked at me.

I tried to move my legs, tried to peel myself from that bed and stop him, because the sight of him in my home, near my Judy, was just too much of an insult. I yelled for him to leave her be and get out, but my voice died in my throat, and suddenly my jaws felt fused together, so I could make no intelligible sounds, just a low-toned mimic of the noises coming from my wife.

His arms went around her, and together, they lifted up. Judy floated out of the chair in Graham's grasp, hovered above the floor. They did a slow, bobbing dance in the air. They rolled forward and then back like a water ballet in a glass tank. Unable to move, I was forced to watch this terrible dance, and that bastard Graham spared me nothing. He brought my Judy across the room and suspended her over the bed only a foot or two from me, so that I saw every line in her stricken face and every red vein in her bewildered eyes. He floated behind her, an arm around her waist and another around her breast, holding my Judy to his body in a position so completely sexual it mocked my god-sworn place as her husband. He clamped his mouth onto her neck. Judy trembled and shook in Graham's arms. A bubble of spit formed at the corner of her mouth, holding tight to her lip like the last air of the drowned.

And then, Graham spoke to me. I don't remember what he said; my head and ears were too full for any simple communication of voice. I wanted to kill him for what he had done, and even more for having made me witness it, but I couldn't move, not even my mouth so that I could curse him.

He left me like that, carrying my Judy out of the house and to the ocean.

8

I had told Clyde that there was no way, no how, that I was going anywhere near the reef when the sun went down.

But as you've maybe already guessed, I did go there.

So, I suppose I'm about as dumb as a rudder myself. But they didn't give me any choice; Claire didn't give me any choice.

The storm had blown through the night before, and a good bit of sun lit up the morning sky. I walked down to the docks, where I said 'Morning' to a couple of the captains who, like myself, were kidding themselves with the idea of impending business. My boat waved hello from her berth as she rode the light morning waves.

A breeze rolled in from the gulf, smelling of salt and the pungent stink of landed weed. Sometimes, when the weed was particularly heavy on the shore, you could barely catch a breath because the air was thick with that backside-of-a-beached-whale stink. But that morning, the air was mostly sweet and calm. The water had a silver cast, all shimmer and invitation.

A Coast Guard tug hauled in a sailing boat. It was one of those twenty-footers favoured by the kids these days, bobbing like a toy in a tub, its sail secured. Its mast had been snapped a few feet from the top. The boat's deck was empty, and I imagined – or maybe *knew* was a better word – that the school hadn't gone hungry the night before.

You hate seeing something like that on such a nice morning, when the water has got a light chop and the sky is as clear as a schoolgirl's eyes, with nothing in it but a wisp of white cloud and a few birds, gulls and terns, gliding over the surf for an easy meal. There's no good time to see a sight like that, but it was looking to be a fine day, and seeing that desolate skiff went a good way to sadden my morning.

While I worked on *Judy Anne*, I got to talking with Reinaldo. Reinaldo was a nice-looking kid from Cuba, who hired out to a few of the different captains when they needed a hand. He knew boats and the water as well as most men twice his age, and you could depend on him to watch your stuff. That's the kind of kid he was; had a lot of integrity, that Reinaldo.

I was scrubbing the deck and polishing the rails, and he was complaining about the way the charters had tapered off over the last few weeks, saying that he needed work soon or his wife would have to go back to waiting tables at Skiff's, a not-so-good restaurant on No Name Key. We didn't talk about the feeders, didn't say a word in speculation as to *why* the charters had dried up. We mostly just talked about the damned shame it all was, particularly since the previous year had been so fine.

When I asked him to join me for a beer around noon, to cut the parch before taking some lunch, Bob Dickinson waddled down the pier, looking like a high seas Santa

Claus with his slicker and boots and a beard whiter than spring clouds.

'Bob,' I said, nodding my head at the captain.

'Reinaldo going out with you today?' Bob asked, his eyes running over the lines of my boat with a bit of jealousy in them. He had himself a fine rig, but I had a classic, and most of the old timers would have sold their wives' souls to have the *Judy Anne* in their slips.

'Not today,' I told him.

'You have a charter?' Reinaldo asked of Bob with a bit of excitement in his voice. 'We going out today?'

'Tonight,' Bob said.

'*Mi Dios*,' Reinaldo said. He crossed himself like a superstitious old woman. But in my opinion, it was the right response. The boy looked at me and then back over the water, toward the western horizon where I'd seen that tug hauling in the empty sailboat only a few hours before.

'Now, come on, Ray,' Bob said. 'You were just over to my boat, asking me for work, and now I'm here, telling you I've got work.'

'Maybe you don't want to go out at night,' I suggested.

'Bah,' Bob scoffed.

The discussion lasted for nearly ten minutes, and Reinaldo finally accepted Bob's offer. The kid had as much pride as he did integrity – damned fine kid. But allowing his caution to be overridden by his need to provide for his family struck me as just plain foolish. I tried to talk him out of it, tried to talk Bob out of it, but things were pretty bad, and any chance to make some honest money had to be taken seriously. Once Reinaldo signed on, I asked Bob about the charter, and you can already guess the three names he told me.

'Timothy Planke. Clyde Hoover.' Then, my heart sank

when he said, 'And that woman from the dress shop on Dolphin Street.'

Claire.

'Did you think to ask why they wanted to go out at night?'

'None of my business,' Bob said. 'And none of yours, either, I imagine.'

I agreed with him on that point; though I was making it my business. The worst kind of people, the scared and desperate sort, were sending themselves out as chum.

And that would have been fine, I suppose. But these desperate people were drawing folks like Bob and Reinaldo into their mess, and that didn't sit well with me.

Growing up in Coral Point, a small place where secrets spread faster than blood on water, you saw the way the town was split between those who worked the docks and those who simply parked their expensive rigs there. It isn't even worth the time to get into what's fair and what's not fair, but I didn't like seeing Planke and his sort buying the lives of good working men, using them up like cigars and dropping the gnawed remnants behind them without the slightest concern.

And that's exactly what was happening. Planke could have skippered his own boat out to the reef, but I couldn't help thinking that the runt was hoping to hire himself not only a vessel, but bait like he'd done with Cole Westman.

Again, I had to question if those folks understood plain English. I knew I had explained the situation, and the outcome was not going to be good. They were going to die. They had about as much chance of coming out of this whole as a wounded albacore in a marlin's mouth. But they were going out, and that was a shame, because it

58

was a beautiful day, and you don't like to think of a beautiful day ending the way that one would.

I still remember Reinaldo's whispered prayers and his final scream. That kind of thing just won't leave your mind once you've heard it; it gets burned in there like the face of your wife, and it stays with you until you're ready for that comfortable bed at the end of your day.

El dios me ayuda!

And I wish his god had helped him, or at least would help him when they met, which I imagine they did about an hour after sundown.

I didn't go out with them on Bob's boat; I powered the *Judy Anne* out past the reef just about an hour before sunset. I'd spent the remainder of my day, those few hours between having my conversation with Bob and Reinaldo and untying the bowline to set out into the gulf, doing the necessary preparation. I made some stakes from hard wood dowelling I picked up over at Pete's Hardware, and he let me use his disk sander in back to grind them down to good points. Once *Judy Anne* was loaded up, I trawled out to the reef, but I didn't drop anchor, because I didn't want to draw any attention to the boat from below. Instead, I let her drift and made a pot of coffee; I did some thinking; I waited.

As the sun disappeared, I sat in the cabin with a cup of coffee and watched the sunset, a sunset that struck me as different from every other sunset I had ever seen, and I started feeling that tension in my gut. You know that feeling when you're completely lost, and you don't think you'll ever find your way home? Maybe you don't. Nowadays it's hard to get really lost, I mean, dangerously lost. But that's how I felt there for a minute, until I started making my mind work.

I guess what struck me as different about this sunset was my own sense of finality, since it was very possibly the last sunset I would ever see. The reds, shot through with streaking oranges and glorious lavender, reflected off the white foam of distant clouds. The sea rolled from the port side, where it carried a perfect reflection of the blue directly above me and subtly darkened until it was a black line at the horizon, where the sky burned its passionate colours. Gulls dived at the surf between my rig and the shore, and the whole scene was one of calm.

Now, it wasn't because I thought it was a brave thing to do that I took my own boat out alone; it was just the opposite, really.

Bob and Reinaldo and their charter were going to come chugging out in the dark, announcing themselves like a fog horn, and a couple of the folks – not Claire, I hoped – would be on the deck, making easy feeding for the school.

The problem with Planke, and Clyde and Claire, I imagined, was that they'd gotten their ideas about the school from their encounters with Graham or from movies. They imagined they were going out to meet a party of suave bastards that slunk and seduced their victims, moving slow and sexy like drugged whores and talking poetry or sweet pillow talk before they tried to attack.

But it didn't work that way. At least, not with feeders.

So, I sat in the cabin, looking to the west, watching the last light fade over the black line of sea, listening to the distant complaints of gulls, the creaking of the boat's hull and the lapping of mother ocean, and I felt the dull panic of being lost, irrevocably disorientated, and I drank my coffee.

The first time I'd ever endured that dreadful lost feeling I had been a kid, fresh on the water. My father, a fisherman with a strong back but no head for rum and whiskey, hired the both of us out to a tuna boat making a run out of Key West. It was storm season, but money was scarce, the way it is now, and the family had to eat. So we were signed on, and I started learning a good deal about the men who culled their livelihood from the waves. Listening to them bark orders at one another while showing a kinder guidance to me, I admired them and could imagine no other life for myself.

We got caught in a gale late in the day, and the storm threw us to a part of the map we would have been better to avoid.

That was when I saw my first school.

The sea and sky had become a single raging quilt, which I observed with an aching awe from the captain's cabin. My father had requested that I be sheltered inside while the crew attended to securing the wave-swept decks, and the captain agreed, gruffly telling me to keep away from the controls if I was going to take up space.

Through the pane of glass, it appeared that the tuna boat had sailed into a great, unlit cavern like the belly of Jonah's whale. Only the belly we had entered was riddled with black cancer coating the lumpy membrane of waves and clouds with a consuming malevolence. Besides the light of the vessel, the only other signs that we had not sailed directly into a great beast's bowel were the occasional flashes of lightning, which lit up the bruised sky surrounding us like agitated nerve endings.

The comfort I had felt all morning and afternoon was shaken away by the violent crash of waves against the hull. The boat took repeated hits, hard and rolling. When lightning flashed, illuminating the tumours and lesions of bloated cloud and spewing sea, that sense of uncompromising disorientation ignited in me, and I wanted my father to come in off the deck and stand near me, so that the proximity of something familiar might chase away my growing fear.

But what I considered absolute fear was only a prelude to the true dread of seeing the school.

They flew in on the crest of a slate grey swell. Like three sailors spat up from the bottom of the sea to rejoin their living mates, the school glided over the white-capped curl to hang suspended against the scrim of wounded-flesh sky. The sense of being lost, truly and dangerously lost, was etched into my chest as cleanly as a tattoo.

The school was small, only three, but seeing them dripping wet against the night sky, with the raging ocean at their backs, their black, shark eyes scanning the decks for food as the wind tore at their hair and their shredded coats, froze the blood in my heart.

They moved fast, having set their eyes on a mate by the name of Lars, a big, Scandinavian son of a bitch who had moved to the States after a bar brawl had made him a fugitive in his own country. Lars had been locking down a hatch. My father was only ten feet away from the big man with the red beard, but neither of them saw the school hovering at their backs. I was in the cabin, screaming my head off, thinking these three foul sailors, somehow able to fly in the harsh weather, were going to take my father from me.

Instead, they took Lars.

They hit him hard. Two of the feeders grabbed him under the arms and sank their teeth into his shoulder; they lifted him into the pelting rain toward the flashing bolts of lightning shooting veins of light through the diseased skin of the clouds. The third flew up to lock its jaws on Lars's throat. A moment later, they were gone, swept away in the gusting rain, leaving my father alone, trembling on the deck.

And in the cabin, I screamed my terror into rain-spattered glass.

Over the next few days, folks around town talked about the unfortunate Lars. They said it was a damned shame that such a good man had to go so young in a fishing accident – because that's what we had been instructed to tell people.

And now it was night, and thinking about Lars, snatched from the deck of an old tuna boat as hopelessly as a sardine plucked from the surf by a gull, was doing me no good. I poured another cup of coffee and looked to the west, where night's maw ate the waves and the sky, and then to the east where a dome of light covered the city of my home.

Though I was grateful that I didn't have to contest with the weather, or navigate through another whale's gut of storm, I wanted to see Bob's boat. I didn't want to be alone on this ocean, not once the school woke.

When I saw old man Planke at the window, I'd been thinking some ridiculous thoughts, forming plans so outlandish as to be comical, as I weighed my chances against the school.

In life, he had been a merciless entrepreneur with a legendary way with the ladies. Handsome, even in his declining years, it was said that Morris Planke had bedded every kind of woman, from the working girls that prowled Duvall Street in Key West to movie starlets, including an encounter with Marilyn Monroe. Tim Planke had inherited almost none of his father's looks and less of his charm; the guy was a sweat stain his father had left on an old shirt, and the arrogant runt knew it.

And there was old Morris Planke, staring through the window of my cabin, no longer handsome and certainly charmless. His long fingers, tipped in jagged nails, splayed over the glass as he pressed his nose to the window not ten feet from my own. His cadaverous face, trenched with pronounced wrinkles and crusted with an accumulation of sea salt, hovered in a white cowl of hair – wet, tangled and streaked with brine.

I dropped my coffee cup and reached down to pick up one of the sharpened stakes at my feet. Others of his kind would be on the deck, but how many?

As I eased across the room to get a look through the round window set high up on the door, Morris Planke slid across the glass as smoothly as a manta ray over ocean sand. His face met mine at the small porthole, blocking my view of the deck beyond, and I gazed into those black, shark eyes and felt the cold of them filling me like water flowing into the lungs of a drowning man.

He hit the door forcefully, sending a boom of thunder through the cabin. I backed away, nearly tripping over the pile of stakes on the cabin's floor. I reached down and lifted a second weapon, just as Morris slammed his hands against the door again. Beyond the porthole, his sunken face, glittering with salt and hunger, pinched as if in pain, revealing two elongated canines that curved back like the fangs of a cobra.

Then, the old man's face was bathed in harsh light as a deep booming horn sounded from the stern.

I hadn't seen Bob's boat approaching; he'd brought her out dark. But he had brought her out, and I was damned grateful for it right then, with old man Planke's face filling my window.

The black eyes regarded me quickly, probably estimating me as a small catch compared to the bounty on the deck of the approaching vessel. A moment later, he was gone. I looked out the glass, and the deck was clear. The school had gone above or below to coordinate their attack.

I opened the door and immediately saw the crowd on Bob's boat. I started yelling and waving, telling them to get below decks and lock the hatches. The three from town, Tim, Clyde and Claire, stood in the centre of the aft deck, looking confused, shooting glances up to the night and down to the water and all around them. Reinaldo crossed himself from his place near the bow. Bob, looking even more like Saint Nick than usual, stood at the wheel of the *Royal Conch* above them all, waving a hand and shouting, 'Who boarded you? Where'd they go?'

The school answered Bob's last spoken question real quick.

Eight of them dived from the sky, gliding low with the dome of light from Coral Point at their backs. They hit Bob fast, yanking him away from the wheel and suspending him over the deck as their faces buried in his bulk. Bob was so confused he made no sound, not when they tore him from the wheel and not when they dropped his dry husk into the waves.

I wasn't surprised to see that Planke's father led the school. The family never seemed at a loss for vision, whether clear or, as was now the case, perversely blurred. Once they'd finished with Bob, the school – three children with sunken, salted faces and five old timers, two women and three men, including the elder Planke – dived back into the sea.

The first thing I had to do, I knew, was get Claire and those men off Bob's boat. These misguided and suddenly terrified people didn't stand a chance, even below decks.

Bob's boat was made of fibreglass, like so many of the newer fishing rigs, and the school would tear through the sides in no time. They could do the same kind of damage to my hull, but the fact that it was constructed of wood might make them cautious. They feared wood on a primal level, knowing their demise could be fabricated from the material.

'You have to board,' I called to Reinaldo, as he seemed the only one on Bob's deck who wasn't panicking or shouting obscenities. He prayed loudly, but nodded his head in understanding, so I threw him a line.

Once we had it tied off, secured so that the *Royal Conch*'s hull hugged mine, the three townsfolk gathered around Reinaldo, who explained how to cross over. I kept my eyes on the water and the sky, knowing my back was exposed, but hoping the school had gotten a bit of the frenzy out of their system on old Bob.

'*Los diablos de la noche*,' Reinaldo chanted frantically as he grasped Claire's arm and steadied her. The hulls drifted away from one another, leaving too wide a gap for Claire to cross.

I threw a look over my shoulder and thought I saw a small face disappear back below the railing on the far side of my deck. A loud crunch echoed up from Bob's hull and, a moment later, his engine died. They were disabling the boat. I'd heard of this. Sometimes, a school would knock out a radio and the engines, laming the vessel so that the crew could be taken over the course of several nights as they drifted silently in the ocean.

But this was the only night that worried me. Claire's

frightened face, looking up at me from the deck of Bob's fishing boat, was my priority.

When the hulls were again coming together, I threw out my hand and grabbed Claire's palm. Tim Planke was backing away from the edge, his head whipping around like a cornered cat, trying to see everything at once. Reinaldo put his hand to Claire's lower back and, with Clyde's help, shoved as I yanked forward. With a tiny squeal, she glided over the gap and onto the deck of the *Judy Anne*.

I put a stake in her trembling hand and told her to watch our backs while I tried to get the men off the *Royal Conch*. 'Come on,' I yelled at Tim Planke, but he kept backing toward the cabin, shooting looks over his shoulders, spinning in tight circles. Reinaldo continued to mumble about his night devils, sprinkling prayers throughout his manic gibberish as we helped Clyde over the gap and onto my deck.

'*Los diablos de la noche*,' Reinaldo whimpered. '*El dios me ayuda!*'

I told Clyde where to find himself a stake and turned back to coax Tim Planke away from the door of Bob's cabin. Another sickening crunch echoed into the night. The school had gone through the hull, and instead of laming Bob's rig, they were sinking her. Already, she was taking on water at the nose.

'Get your ass over here,' I bellowed, but Planke was trembling, searching the sky for his father.

'Okay, Reinaldo,' I said, 'You first.'

'The man,' Reinaldo said, pointing over his shoulder at Planke.

'You first,' I told him.

When the hulls came close again, Reinaldo put his foot

on the railing and locked his hand in mine, but the gap hadn't completely closed.

The child feeders, three little demons, shot from the water between the boats. One hit Reinaldo in the crotch, rocketing the boy five feet above my head, while the other two went for his neck. The kid between Reinaldo's legs turned his head and bit into the artery running through the thigh. When the feeder clamped his jaws, his eyes rolled back with the ecstasy of his meal.

'*El dios me ayuda!*' Reinaldo screamed. '*El dios ...*'

The child feeders dived, pulling Reinaldo between the boats, right past my face and back into the black water. Then, the hulls thumped together in a dull embrace before a new gap opened.

Reinaldo's fate sent Tim Planke to the cabin of Bob's boat. I kept hollering at him to hurry up while they were feeding and to get away from that door, but my warnings were lost on him. His mind had snapped in just under a second when he'd seen those kids latch onto Reinaldo.

And as is often the case, his panic killed him.

He opened the door to the cabin and they launched out of the darkness, hitting his chest like a cannonball.

Leading the pack of old timers was Planke's father, shooting out of the cabin like a torpedo. He hit his son's chest so hard that I heard the spine and ribs snap in the crisp night air. Father and son rocketed halfway across the deck before they came to a stuttering halt. I thought I heard Planke, his voice as small as a child's, say, 'Daddy.' But then the other three were on him.

Bones and cartilage snapped, and the wet sounds of smacking lips and sucking rolled over the deck before the school glided back into the black mouth of the cabin, leaving the deck of the *Royal Conch* desolate as her nose continued to dip into the waves.

Quickly, I untied the line and threw it onto the deserted deck of Bob's rig. Behind me, Claire screamed, and I spun to find that the children had finished with Reinaldo.

The three child feeders, siblings of Graham's infection, hung suspended against the night. The boys' suits and the girl's dress, damp and frayed from the attention of aquatic scavengers, blew on the light breeze. Their faces, ragged masks with pinpoint eyes, gazed down on us with curiosity. Their hunger had been temporarily sated, but they were a greedy kind, and already they were considering what they might do with the food cowering on the deck before them.

Wound the ship or wound the prey, I thought. Those were their only options. If they breached *Judy Anne*'s hull, then they could wait until morning, just before sunrise, to take the rest of us. I looked for some humanity in those tiny faces, something like pity, I suppose. But the children wore matching expressions of calculation, like lions assessing a herd of antelope.

And of course, they saw Claire as the weakness in our herd.

They dived from the stern in a delta formation, like a grouping of Antillean nighthawks, while opening their mouths to reveal their feeding teeth. Claire screamed as I shoved her to the deck. Beside me, Clyde let out a low groan and lifted the pointed dowel, and together we formed a wall in front of Claire. Clyde took the worst of the first attack, squirming and shouting as he stabbed at the body of the boy that tried to latch onto his neck.

The boy in his burial suit and the little girl with the once-blue dress came for me, but fear had numbed me and clarified my senses. When they struck, one to a shoulder, I was already in motion, driving the point of the stake upward. The fabric of the dress and the flesh beneath parted easily before the sharp tip, and even as the little girl tried to taste me, the stake shattered her ribs and pierced her heart.

The child didn't scream. Instead, she went limp on the point, and I dropped her to the deck while I turned my attention to the boy, scraping his nails over my shirt to open skin and fabric.

Through this brief attack, I kept thinking that we had to hurry, had to get inside before the elders finished with Tim Planke in the flooded hull of Bob's boat. Panic gave me competence. I pivoted on my foot and charged forward, slamming the boy's body into the solid wooden wall of the cabin. The impact dazed the little bastard and he wriggled away to take to the air.

Clyde had dropped his stake and was in a strangling match with the little kid that had locked his legs around his torso as his nails buried in Clyde's neck. I cast a look to the sky, finding the boy hovering above the cabin, watching the scene below with his pinpoint eyes.

Then a piercing wail, part animal and part human terror, peeled out, and Claire rose from the deck. She drove her stake into the little boy's back with a feral cry and then stumbled back, trembling so badly that her whole body twitched, shuddering violently, perhaps to rid herself of what she had done.

But her strike, while distracting the child, had missed its mark. I stepped forward and pulled the post free, took aim and plunged the stake into the boy's back. A rib snapped in dislocation to accommodate the wood's girth, and then he joined his sister on the deck.

I ushered the panicked Claire and bleeding Clyde into

the cabin. We each took another weapon from the floor, though I felt Claire, and possibly Clyde, were beyond using them. At the window, I checked Bob's boat for movement, but saw nothing but the wedge of water creeping over her deck as she sank.

Surely they'd be done with Planke by now.

'So fast,' Clyde whispered, wrapping a handkerchief around his neck to bandage the cuts there. 'They're so damned fast.'

'Close the door,' Claire cried, pointing a trembling finger at the opening. 'Close the door.'

But I wanted the door open. I wanted the feeders to think they had a way in, so we could take them one at a time, instead of having them swarm through the glass at our backs. Claire took a jerking step forward to shut us in, and I put my hand on her shoulder. I shook my head.

At the console, I turned on the fog lights and the deck lights, sending an aureole of illumination over the deck and the water. Above the cabin, I heard the boy make a sound like a wounded gull. The squawk was followed by a heavy splash to the port side as the tainted child sought the darkness below the waves.

'What are we going to do?' Clyde asked.

But that wasn't the important question. The important question was; what were *they* going to do?

Claire touched my shoulder, that poor woman. Her face asked the same question as Clyde, only it did so with infinitely greater force, despite the fact she said nothing.

'Guard the door,' I told them both.

Once they were taking their positions across the cabin, I brought the engines to life and set out to skirt the wreck at our side before attempting to make a run for the shore.

Through the glass, over the bow, in the dull green glow of the ocean, I saw them. The school had regrouped just below the waves. Looking like a smack of jellyfish, their pale faces barely submerged, the remnants of the school looked on as the sea parted in front of my boat. Just before the bow eclipsed them, they sank from view, the white disks of their faces dissolving into the murky green water.

I didn't breathe for the next several seconds as I knew they had a clear shot at the hull. If I could keep the boat moving, we stood a chance.

They didn't go for the hull, and for a few seconds, I tried to convince myself that they were done with us. After all, they'd had a good night's meal – Bob, Reinaldo and Tim Planke made a fine haul. Still, I realised this hope was the hope of the desperate, the irrevocably lost, like the fantasies I'd created before seeing the elder Planke at my cabin's window.

'How do we explain these kids?' Clyde called over my shoulder.

Apparently, he was convinced the threat had passed, if his mind had already moved onto practical matters, such as explaining ourselves to the authorities. He did raise a good point, but it hardly seemed relevant when we had a good thirty-minute trawl back to shore; that was a damned long time in our situation. From the moment I first saw Planke at my window, until I started the engines, less than thirty minutes had passed. And sure we'd brought down two of the small ones, but we were a long way from being in the clear.

'Leave them on the deck, for now,' I told him.

I left the wheel and joined them at the door of the cabin, my eyes searching the glowing water gliding like a halo around the hull and the darkness beyond. Stars twinkled in the distant sky, indifferent to the struggle below them. Next to me, Claire breathed quietly, holding a hand over her chest as if to support the ribs, against which her heart thundered. Clyde shifted his weight from foot to foot, a subtle dance of panic.

'How many are left?' Clyde asked.

'Six,' I told him. 'One kid and five old timers.'

'Six,' Claire sighed.

Retrieving two more stakes from the middle of the cabin and shoving them into my pockets, I asked Clyde if he could handle the boat. He took his place by the wheel; I crossed the cabin to the door, where Claire stopped me.

'I'm just going to check above. We're blind up there, and I don't like this quiet.'

'You shouldn't go out there,' Claire said, and I almost stopped, because I could see that she was taking my actions as bravery, and it seemed to hurt her, which was so kind it made my heart shudder.

'If they're over the cabin, then we need to know it. They can attack us any time they choose, and we should be ready for it.'

That was only part of the truth, the part I could bring myself to speak. I couldn't tell Claire about my need to keep her safe, a need that seemed to come from a place deep in my chest. This place had been well worn by similar feelings for my Judy.

Warm night air settled in around me, swaddling me against the fearful, slightly disbelieving look Claire had fixed on my back. Once I cleared the eaves, I threw a glance upward to check the sky above the cabin, but none of the feeders was there.

Thinking back, I can only guess that they had latched themselves to the side of my boat like a colony of barnacles, waiting for this moment. I hadn't made it four steps onto the deck before they struck.

I didn't see which ones grabbed me; there might have been two or three. Suddenly, the deck was pulling away, and I was being dragged feet first into the air. Momentary confusion sufficiently blocked the pain of their teeth in my legs. My hands flew out to find purchase on something, anything to keep from the complete helplessness that the sky above promised.

My hands found the eaves of the flydeck, and I clutched with the strength of blind panic. Something popped loudly in my ear, my shoulder dislocating from the socket, but I didn't let go.

Their nails dragged over my calves, leaving deep trenches in the meat, but the sudden resistance took them off guard. They continued into the sky, pieces of my pants and legs under their nails and filling their mouths, but I jerked free and slammed onto the deck, landing flat on my back.

Though stunned, I sought out one of the dowels. I freed it from my pocket and was frozen by what hovered over me.

I stared straight up and into the face of the elder Planke. A small crab, tangled in the old man's hair, broke free and dropped onto my chest, where it scurried to my belly before dropping to the deck. The old man's mouth opened in a soulless appreciation of the meal I had become.

Planke dropped quickly, right onto the point of the post in my hand. He spat a tide of bloody salt water into my face, blinding me as his teeth sought out my throat. Then my two passengers followed my example and pierced his body with their stakes. Made blind by the salty discharge, I didn't know if Claire or Clyde had made the killing blow, but I felt the weight of Old Man Planke hit me hard and then roll away.

Somewhere, not far from me, Claire was screaming. I wiped the foul fluid from my eyes and blinked until I could see.

They had poor Clyde. Three of the old ones were latched onto the man; they all hovered only a few feet off the deck, but didn't seem interested in feeding on their prey. They just wanted to disassemble him, which they did with terrible speed.

Clyde couldn't scream, because his throat had been torn out; a divot of meat dangled over the rapidly spreading stain on his polo shirt. One of the elders bit into the shoulder and spat the meat onto the deck. Another plunged the sharp nails of its thumbs into Clyde's eye sockets, grinding the delicate orbs to pulp in their nests. A third worked over Clyde's leg, wrenching the limb in tight circles as if to unscrew it from the socket. When the thigh parted from the hip amid a shower of blood and urine, the feeder took to the air, flying straight up toward the stars, swinging the appendage like an oar before discarding it. Clyde's other limbs were treated similarly until the husk of his torso hit the deck with a dull thud. The last of the child feeders dived low, and as a final humiliation wrenched Clyde's skull from his body. Ligament and muscle snapped until the upper half of Clyde's head came free, leaving a bloated, useless tongue to nestle behind the fence of his lower teeth as blood and spinal discharge pooled about the shoulders.

They had finished feeding for the night; this violence was meant to be a warning or perhaps revenge for what we had done to the school. *You can't win*, they seemed to say. *Look at our strength – our power. We rule the night and the waves, and this is what comes of challenging us.* All this I read in their hateful faces as the school drew back toward the horizon, leaving the token of their threat in a bloody pile on the deck of the *Judy Anne*.

And Claire continued screaming.

9

You might remember that early on I mentioned an old saying that goes: if you travel far enough in any direction, you'll end up right back where you started.

Coral Point is still there. Her depleted population continues to wonder at the number of folks lost at sea, and tourists pretty much avoid the place now. Tib's went out of business as her clientele waned and then vanished completely, either disappearing into the gulf or moving away from the haunted waters.

I healed up pretty good. Every now and then my shoulder gives me some aches and pains, but I can still captain a boat.

Claire has a different tale to tell.

She still wakes up screaming. During the days, she wanders around like she left a piece of her mind back on the deck of the *Judy Anne*. She doesn't say much, just nods her head and spends a lot of time staring out of windows. When the sun starts to set, she closes the blinds and the curtains, and she stays close to me. But sometimes I feel like she isn't there at all, even when her nails dig into my arm because she thinks she's heard a noise on the back porch.

After the night her friends died, Claire couldn't bear to be away from me, but it wasn't the kind of companionship I had hoped for. Fear, not love, fastened her to my side, though for a time, I convinced myself that her affection was genuine.

Even a guy dumb as a rudder would understand that I loved her something terrible. Nothing else could have driven me out on the water that night. Like a schoolboy trying to impress a cheerleader with some foolish stunt, I'd imagined that I could turn her head with an act that I wanted to call bravery.

We married a few months after that night on the *Judy Anne*, and I do what I can for her. Still, Claire's fear and pain make me think about my first wife.

And thinking about their pain, Claire's pain and Judy's pain, makes me think back many years, four years before the beginning of this story, to the day I asked a fellow by the name of Graham to stop my Judy's suffering.

That was the truth behind the lie I'd told Clyde Hoover over at Ethel's on a cloudy afternoon when he'd wanted to play Sherlock Holmes with me. I'd told him that Graham had approached me, made me engage him in conversation and ultimately invite him to a doomed meeting with my wife. The truth was, I had sought Graham out, knowing his nature and knowing that he could help my Judy find peace.

I couldn't do it myself. I could never lay hands on my Judy in a way that would hurt her, but that damned suffering, the misery I had to watch day after day, was just too much for my heart to bear. So, I found Graham and begged for his help.

Graham only did what I'd wanted him to do, but I hated him for it. Graham wore the face of my guilt – a rugged, cold face that I could not look at without seeing my own corruption. Maybe that's why I exposed Graham to Planke and the others when he returned to Coral Point. I was in Graham's debt, but god how I wanted him to pay for the favour he had done me.

The irony doesn't escape me. After all, Planke went out and hired Cole Westman and some other men to kill Graham. Planke did exactly what I'd wanted him to do. He didn't wait for Graham to finish his business, didn't wait for the harvest, but he did kill him. As a result, I got closer to the woman who would become my second wife, and here I am thinking about her pain. And I find myself wondering what I can do to stop her suffering, the way I did with Judy. So, I suppose I've gone all the way around the globe.

But like I said, most of us don't navigate very well, so we keep pushing on in the same direction.

And then, dumb as rudders, we act surprised when we end up right back where we started.

About The Author

Lee Thomas is the Bram Stoker Award-Nominated author of the novel *Stained*. His short fiction has appeared in dozens of publications, including the anthologies *Darkside III: A Walk on the Darkside* and *The Book of Final Flesh*. Lee lives in New York City where he is currently working on a new novel and several short works of fiction. Visit him on the web at www.leethomasauthor.com.

Acknowledgements

For all of their help in getting this project to publication, thanks to Pete Allen, Megan Bulloch, Kealan Patrick Burke, Nicholas Kaufmann, Mark McLaughlin and Joseph Nassise.

For their ongoing support, friendship and inspiration, many thanks to Linda Addison, Daniel Braum, P D Cacek, Kris Dikeman, Gerard Houarner, Jack Ketchum, Gregory Lamberson, Sarah Langan, Jane Osnovich, K Z Perry, and Stefan Petrucha.

Special thanks to Matt Schwartz and Shocklines.com, the premier outlet for all things horror on the web.

Other Telos Titles Available

TIME HUNTER

A range of high-quality, original paperback and limited edition hardback novellas featuring the adventures in time of Honoré Lechasseur. Part mystery, part detective story, part dark fantasy, part science fiction ... these books are guaranteed to enthral fans of good fiction everywhere, and are in the spirit of our acclaimed range of *Doctor Who* Novellas.

ALREADY AVAILABLE

THE WINNING SIDE by LANCE PARKIN
Emily is dead! Killed by an unknown assailant. Honoré and Emily find themselves caught up in a plot reaching from the future to their past, and with their very existence, not to mention the future of the entire world, at stake, can they unravel the mystery before it is too late?
An adventure in time and space.
£7.99 (+ £1.50 UK p&p) Standard p/b ISBN 1-903889-35-9 (pb)

THE TUNNEL AT THE END OF THE LIGHT
by STEFAN PETRUCHA
In the heart of post-war London, a bomb is discovered lodged at a disused station between Green Park and Hyde Park Corner. The bomb detonates, and as the dust clears, it becomes apparent that *something* has been awakened. Strange half-human creatures attack the workers at the site,

hungrily searching for anything containing sugar …

Meanwhile, Honoré and Emily are contacted by eccentric poet Randolph Crest, who believes himself to be the target of these subterranean creatures. The ensuing investigation brings Honoré and Emily up against a terrifying force from deep beneath the earth, and one which even with their combined powers, they may have trouble stopping.

An adventure in time and space.

£7.99 (+ £1.50 UK p&p) Standard p/b ISBN 1-903889-37-5 (pb)
£25.00 (+ £1.50 UK p&p) Deluxe h/b ISBN 1-903889-38-3 (hb)

THE CLOCKWORK WOMAN by CLAIRE BOTT
Honoré and Emily find themselves imprisoned in the 19th Century by a celebrated inventor … but help comes from an unexpected source – a humanoid automaton created by and to give pleasure to its owner. As the trio escape to London, they are unprepared for what awaits them, and at every turn it seems impossible to avert what fate may have in store for the Clockwork Woman.

An adventure in time and space.

£7.99 (+ £1.50 UK p&p) Standard p/b ISBN 1-903889-39-1 (pb)
£25.00 (+ £1.50 UK p&p) Deluxe h/b ISBN 1-903889-40-5 (hb)

KITSUNE by JOHN PAUL CATTON
In the year 2020, Honoré and Emily find themselves thrown into a mystery, as an ice spirit – *Yuki-Onna* – wreaks havoc during the Kyoto Festival, and a haunted funhouse proves to contain more than just paper lanterns and wax dummies. But what does all this have to do with the elegant owner of the Hide and Chic fashion chain … and to the legendary Chinese fox-spirits, the Kitsune?

An adventure in time and space.

£7.99 (+ £1.50 UK p&p) Standard p/b ISBN 1-903889-41-3 (pb)
£25.00 (+ £1.50 UK p&p) Deluxe h/b ISBN 1-903889-42-1 (hb)

THE SEVERED MAN by GEORGE MANN
What links a clutch of sinister murders in Victorian London, an angel appearing in a Staffordshire village in the 1920s and a small boy running loose around the capital in 1950? When Honoré and Emily encounter a man who appears to have been cut out of time, they think they have the answer. But soon enough they discover that the mystery is only just beginning and that nightmares can turn into reality.
An adventure in time and space.
£7.99 (+ £1.50 UK p&p) Standard p/b ISBN 1-903889-43-X (pb)
£25.00 (+ £1.50 UK p&p) Deluxe h/b ISBN 1-903889-44-8 (hb)

ECHOES
by IAIN MCLAUGHLIN & CLAIRE BARTLETT
Echoes of the past ... echoes of the future. Honoré Lechasseur can see the threads that bind the two together, however when he and Emily Blandish find themselves outside the imposing tower-block headquarters of Dragon Industry, both can sense something is wrong. There are ghosts in the building, and images and echoes of all times pervade the structure. But what is behind this massive contradiction in time, and can Honoré and Emily figure it out before they become trapped themselves ...?
An adventure in time and space.
£7.99 (+ £1.50 UK p&p) Standard p/b ISBN 1-903889-45-6 (pb)
£25.00 (+ £1.50 UK p&p) Deluxe h/b ISBN 1-903889-46-4 (hb)

PECULIAR LIVES by PHILIP PURSER-HALLARD
Once a celebrated author of 'scientific romances', Erik

Clevedon is an old man now. But his fiction conceals a dangerous truth, as Honoré Lechasseur and Emily Blandish discover after a chance encounter with a strangely gifted young pickpocket. Born between the Wars, the superhuman children known as 'the Peculiar' are reaching adulthood – and they believe that humanity is making a poor job of looking after the world they plan to inherit ...

An adventure in time and space.

£7.99 (+ £1.50 UK p&p) Standard p/b ISBN 1-903889-47-2 (pb)
£25.00 (+ £1.50 UK p&p) Deluxe h/b ISBN 1-903889-48-0 (hb)

TIME HUNTER FILM

DAEMOS RISING
by DAVID J HOWE, DIRECTED BY KEITH BARNFATHER

Daemos Rising is a sequel to both the *Doctor Who* adventure *The Daemons* and to *Downtime*, an earlier drama featuring the Yeti. It is also a prequel of sorts to Telos Publishing's *Time Hunter* series. It stars Miles Richardson as ex-UNIT operative Douglas Cavendish, and Beverley Cressman as Brigadier Lethbridge-Stewart's daughter Kate. Trapped in an isolated cottage, Cavendish thinks he is seeing ghosts. The only person who might understand and help is Kate Lethbridge-Stewart … but when she arrives, she realises that Cavendish is key in a plot to summon the Daemons back to the Earth. With time running out, Kate discovers that sometimes even the familiar can turn out to be your worst nightmare. Also starring Andrew Wisher, and featuring Ian Richardson as the Narrator.

An adventure in time and space.

£14.00 (+ £2.50 UK p&p) PAL format R4 DVD

Order direct from Reeltime Pictures, PO Box 23435, London SE26 5WU

HORROR/FANTASY

CAPE WRATH by PAUL FINCH
Death and horror on a deserted Scottish island as an
ancient Viking warrior chief returns to life.
£8.00 (+ £1.50 UK p&p) Standard p/b ISBN: 1-903889-60-X

KING OF ALL THE DEAD
by STEVE LOCKLEY & PAUL LEWIS
The king of all the dead will have what is his.
£8.00 (+ £1.50 UK p&p) Standard p/b ISBN: 1-903889-61-8

GUARDIAN ANGEL by STEPHANIE BEDWELL-GRIME
Devilish fun as Guardian Angel Porsche Winter loses a soul
to the devil ...
£9.99 (+ £2.50 UK p&p) Standard p/b ISBN: 1-903889-62-6

FALLEN ANGEL by STEPHANIE BEDWELL-GRIME
Porsche Winter battles she devils on Earth ...
£9.99 (+ £2.50 UK p&p) Standard p/b ISBN: 1-903889-69-3

ASPECTS OF A PSYCHOPATH by ALISTAIR LANGSTON
Goes deeper than ever before into the twisted psyche of a
serial killer. Horrific, graphic and gripping, this book is not
for the squeamish.
£8.00 (+ £1.50 UK p&p) Standard p/b ISBN: 1-903889-63-4

SPECTRE by STEPHEN LAWS
The inseparable Byker Chapter: six boys, one girl, growing
up together in the back streets of Newcastle. Now
memories are all that Richard Eden has left, and one
treasured photograph. But suddenly, inexplicably, the
images of his companions start to fade, and as they vanish,

so his friends are found dead and mutilated. Something is stalking the Chapter, picking them off one by one, something connected with their past, and with the girl they used to know.
£9.99 (+ £2.50 UK p&p) Standard p/b ISBN: 1-903889-72-3

THE HUMAN ABSTRACT by GEORGE MANN
A future tale of private detectives, AIs, Nanobots, love and death.
£7.99 (+ £1.50 UK p&p) Standard p/b ISBN: 1-903889-65-0

BREATHE by CHRISTOPHER FOWLER
The Office meets *Night of the Living Dead.*
£7.99 (+ £1.50 UK p&p) Standard p/b ISBN: 1-903889-67-7
£25.00 (+ £1.50 UK p&p) Deluxe h/b ISBN: 1-903889-68-5

HOUDINI'S LAST ILLUSION by STEVE SAVILE
Can the master illusionist Harry Houdini outwit the dead shades of his past?
£7.99 (+ £1.50 UK p&p) Standard p/b ISBN: 1-903889-66-9

ALICE'S JOURNEY BEYOND THE MOON
by R J CARTER
A sequel to the classic Lewis Carroll tales.
£6.99 (+ £1.50 UK p&p) Standard p/b ISBN: 1-903889-76-6
£30.00 (+ £1.50 UK p&p) Deluxe h/b ISBN: 1-903889-77-4

APPROACHING OMEGA by ERIC BROWN
A colonisation mission to Earth runs into problems.
£7.99 (+ £1.50 UK p&p) Standard p/b ISBN: 1-903889-98-7
£30.00 (+ £1.50 UK p&p) Deluxe h/b ISBN: 1-903889-99-5

VALLEY OF LIGHTS by STEPHEN GALLAGHER
A cop comes up against a body-hopping murderer …
£9.99 (+ £2.50 UK p&p) Standard p/b ISBN: 1-903889-74-X
£30.00 (+ £2.50 UK p&p) Deluxe h/b ISBN: 1-903889-75-8

TV/FILM GUIDES

A DAY IN THE LIFE: THE UNOFFICIAL AND
UNAUTHORISED GUIDE TO 24 by KEITH TOPPING
Complete episode guide to the first season of the popular
TV show.
£9.99 (+ £2.50 p&p) Standard p/b ISBN: 1-903889-53-7

THE TELEVISION COMPANION: THE UNOFFICIAL
AND UNAUTHORISED GUIDE TO DOCTOR WHO
by DAVID J HOWE & STEPHEN JAMES WALKER
Complete episode guide (1963 – 1996) to the popular TV
show.
£14.99 (+ £4.75 UK p&p) Standard p/b ISBN: 1-903889-51-0

LIBERATION: THE UNOFFICIAL AND UNAUTHORISED
GUIDE TO BLAKE'S 7
by ALAN STEVENS & FIONA MOORE
Complete episode guide to the popular TV show.
Featuring a foreword by David Maloney
£9.99 (+ £2.50 UK p&p) Standard p/b ISBN: 1-903889-54-5

HOWE'S TRANSCENDENTAL TOYBOX: SECOND
EDITION
by DAVID J HOWE & ARNOLD T BLUMBERG
Complete guide to Doctor Who Merchandise.
£25.00 (+ £4.75 UK p&p) Standard p/b ISBN: 1-903889-56-1

HOWE'S TRANSCENDENTAL TOYBOX: UPDATE No
1: 2003 by DAVID J HOWE & ARNOLD T BLUMBERG
Complete guide to Doctor Who Merchandise released in
2003.
£7.99 (+ £1.50 UK p&p) Standard p/b ISBN: 1-903889-57-X

A VAULT OF HORROR by KEITH TOPPING
A guide to 80 classic (and not so classic) British Horror Films.
£12.99 (+ £4.75 UK p&p) Standard p/b ISBN: 1-903889-58-8

BEAUTIFUL MONSTERS: THE UNOFFICIAL AND UNAUTHORISED GUIDE TO THE ALIEN AND PREDATOR FILMS by DAVID McINTEE
A guide to the Alien and Predator Films.
£9.99 (+ £2.50 UK p&p) Standard p/b ISBN: 1-903889-94-4

THE HANDBOOK: THE UNOFFICIAL AND UNAUTHORISED GUIDE TO THE PRODUCTION OF DOCTOR WHO
by DAVID J HOWE, STEPHEN JAMES WALKER and MARK STAMMERS
Complete guide to the making of Doctor Who (1963 – 1996).
£14.99 (+ £4.75 UK p&p) Standard p/b ISBN: 1-903889-59-6
£30.00 (+ £4.75 UK p&p) Deluxe h/b ISBN: 1-903889-96-0

HANK JANSON

Classic pulp crime thrillers from the 1940s and 1950s.

TORMENT by HANK JANSON
£9.99 (+ £1.50 UK p&p) Standard p/b ISBN: 1-903889-80-4
WOMEN HATE TILL DEATH by HANK JANSON
£9.99 (+ £1.50 UK p&p) Standard p/b ISBN: 1-903889-81-2
SOME LOOK BETTER DEAD by HANK JANSON
£9.99 (+ £1.50 UK p&p) Standard p/b ISBN: 1-903889-82-0
SKIRTS BRING ME SORROW by HANK JANSON
£9.99 (+ £1.50 UK p&p) Standard p/b ISBN: 1-903889-83-9
WHEN DAMES GET TOUGH by HANK JANSON
£9.99 (+ £1.50 UK p&p) Standard p/b ISBN: 1-903889-85-5
ACCUSED by HANK JANSON
£9.99 (+ £1.50 UK p&p) Standard p/b ISBN: 1-903889-86-3
KILLER by HANK JANSON
£9.99 (+ £1.50 UK p&p) Standard p/b ISBN: 1-903889-87-1
FRAILS CAN BE SO TOUGH by HANK JANSON
£9.99 (+ £1.50 UK p&p) Standard p/b ISBN: 1-903889-88-X
BROADS DON'T SCARE EASY by HANK JANSON
£9.99 (+ £1.50 UK p&p) Standard p/b ISBN: 1-903889-89-8
KILL HER IF YOU CAN by HANK JANSON
£9.99 (+ £1.50 UK p&p) Standard p/b ISBN: 1-903889-90-1

Non-fiction

THE TRIALS OF HANK JANSON by STEVE HOLLAND
£12.99 (+ £2.50 UK p&p) Standard p/b ISBN: 1-903889-84-7

The prices shown are correct at time of going to press. However, the publishers reserve the right to increase prices from those previously advertised without prior notice.

TELOS PUBLISHING
c/o Beech House, Chapel Lane, Moulton, Cheshire, CW9
8PQ, England
Email: orders@telos.co.uk
Web: www.telos.co.uk

To order copies of any Telos books, please visit our website where there are full details of all titles and facilities for worldwide credit card online ordering, or send a cheque or postal order (UK only) for the appropriate amount (including postage and packing), together with details of the book(s) you require, plus your name and address to the above address. Overseas readers please send two international reply coupons for details of prices and postage rates.